ISBN: 978-0-9556863-0-6
Published by Fundays Enterprises Ltd (R) 2007

Fundays Enterprises Ltd (R) Registered Office:
Somerset House 40-49 Price Street, Birmingham,
B4 6LZ

I0681815

Cover design by Ansar

This is a semi-factual poetic play based primarily upon accounts
of Cyrus' life offered by Herodoctus' in his Histories
and Xenophon's Cyropaedia.
Hopefully you will find it an enjoyable enough read that it will ignite the
flame of curiosity in you to discover more about this great king yourself.
For Cyrus deserves to be remembered as one of history's truly Great
emperors, the one who inspired Alexander by building an empire that can
be termed truly mighty, magnificent and multi-cultural with many nations
and peoples under its vassalage

For the most wondrous and gentle soul ever
that I call my mother
Bibi Ghulam Raza

Cyrus

Q Shah

List of Characters in Alphabetical Order

Abradatas of Susa: Babylonian vassal
Adish: Persian tribal leader
Araspas: Median Noble/ Cyrus' friend from time in Ecbatan
Arasha: Cyrus' childhood friend
Artabazus: Cyrus' Median General/Friend
Artembares: Astyages' kin
Artagerses: Cyrus' camel cavalry commander
Astyages: King of Media
Babylonian Noble: At Balshazzar's feast
Bahador – Captain of Astyages Royal Guard
Balshazzar: King Nabonidus' son and co-regent of Babylonia
Balshazzar's Queen
Banquet Announcer: (at Astyages' Palace)
Byarshan: Cyrus' childhood friend
Cambyses: King of Anshan/Cyrus' father
Cambyses: Cyrus' elder son
Chief Soothsayer: of Babylon
Chrysantas: Persian general/nobleman
Croesus: King of Lydia
Croesus' Agent
Cyno: Lydian/Mitradates' wife/Cyrus' foster mother
Cyrus (Kasra as named by his foster parents**):** First Achaemenid Emperor
Daniel: Hebrew Prophet
Darioush: Captain of Cyrus' Royal Palace Guards
Dratha: Cyrus' childhood friend
Erexsha: Cyrus' childhood friend
Franya: Cyrus' childhood friend
Gadatas: Disaffected Babylonian nobleman
Gobyras: Disaffected Babylonian nobleman
Gubaru: Median Noble/Governor of Gutium/Cyrus' general
Harpagus: Astyages kin/Cyrus' general and confidant
Humaya: Harpagus' wife
Hystaspas: Persian noble/ Cyrus' general
Jamshid: Persian sergeant
Mandane: daughter of Astyages/wife of Cambyses/mother of Cyrus
Mitradates: Lydian/ Astyages' farmer/Cyrus' foster father
Nabonidus: Emperor of Babylonia
Narrator
Nargis: Panthea's lady-in-waiting
Pantheia of Susa: wife of Lord Abradatas
Pharnuchus: Cyrus' infantry commander
Rostam: Captain of Cyrus' palace guard
Sadanis: Lydian Elder
Sama: Artembares' son
Smerdis: Cyrus' younger son

Tigranes: Prince of Armenia/Cyrus' friend from time in Ecbatan
Tomyris: Queen of The Massagetae
Zavan: Chief Magi of Media
Xerxes: Persian General
Peyam; Harpagus' messenger to Cyrus

Contents

5

Cyrus
Prologue

Around 2600 years ago in the ancient city of Ecbatan,
Was born a child to the Royal Persian House of Anshan,
son of Cambyses a just and noble king,
and Mandane a gentle and beautiful queen,
daughter of Astyages the Median tyrant king,
bore Cyrus the greatest emperor ever seen.

The first Achaemenid Emperor,
Cyrus was a most humble and upright ruler
destined to be the greatest emperor
to ever grace the world's stage.
Excelled he in compassion and intelligence,
a strong and gentle soul who never countenanced anger or rage.
Abhorred did he people of sloth, disloyalty and wicked sense.

On the death of his father Cambyses,
bequeathed was he a small impoverished kingdom
the city-state Anshan, a vassal of the Median Emperor Astyages.
The Persians were the model of civilized admiration,
from peasant to king, observed all the rule of law,
equality prevailed, till Cyrus was no more.

From the king of a humble and rugged city-state,
Cyrus became liege of powerful Media,
with the consent of its grateful citizenry,
who revolted and sealed brutal Astyages' fate.
Soon after, he conquered the great empires of wealthy Lydia,
and Old Babylonia with its cultural grace so mighty

And on his dying breath his son Cambyses, did he leave
a vast and diverse empire, the like of which had never before been,
Stretching thousands of miles in each and every direction,
from Arabia in the South to the northern Black Sea,
Lydia in the West to Gandhara in the East the most glorious ever seen,
with peoples, races and tongues too numerous to mention.

Cyrus' rule was a model of deference and tolerance
for one's fellow man irrespective of race religion or creed.
All the differing peoples of his empire remained unencumbered,
to practice their religions and laws unfettered.
Treated were all equally, his vassals the same as his Persian breed.
Ushered he a reign of benevolence
not of terror and malevolence.

A Father, A Law Bringer, A Liberator, An Anointed Soul was he,
who freed the weak from the bonds of servitude and abolished slavery.
Commanded he such love and affection by his graciousness
that, many who never did him see,
felt indebted loyalty
for his kindness.

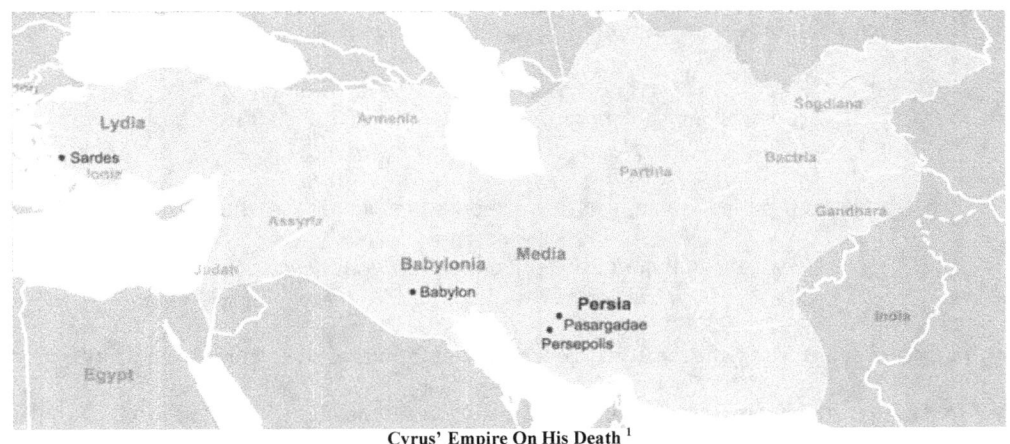

Cyrus' Empire On His Death [1]

[1] map from: http://en.wikipedia.org/wiki/Image:Persia-Cyrus2-World3.png

Act One – Part I
592 BC - King Astyages' Vision

(In the private quarters of King Astyages of Media's palace in Ecbatan enter the Chief Magi Zavan)

Zavan: Afternoon My Lord, I came as quickly as my old legs could carry
but I am forever imposed for my manifold religious duties by all and sundry.

Astyages: Yes, yes Zavan, don't worry
I won't punish your tardiness …THIS TIME I shall let it be.
(He speaks in a menacing taunt)

I am troubled Zavan, what I am about to recount is for your ears only!
And I mean that most seriously!
Otherwise I shall not hesitate in cutting off your head …. Personally!
(His voice in raised in mortal threat)

Zavan: Sire, you can always count on me for utmost discretion and loyalty.

Astyages: Judging by the rumours that prevail around the court I am sure magi … you are
indeed the seal of secrecy!

Zavan: Sire, how could you say such a thing, you know well we the Magi,
are a spiritual lot sworn to confidentiality.
(He protests profusely)

Astyages: Yes .. yes .. I am sure – anyway enough of this gibber gabber.
Let me recount the matter
that troubles me each and every night …
and see if your so called gift of prophesy can throw some light.

For a few weeks now I've had a recurrent dream.
Each night I see from my sweet Mandane flow a stream
that comes first to fill my Ecbatan and then the whole of Asia.
Now tell me what are your thoughts on the matter?

Zavan: Well sire ….. I am afraid it portents ill
forgive my candidness but as a humble servant who always will ….

9

Astyages: For heaven's sake Zavan, enough of this humble servitude!
Just interpret the truth!

(Choosing his words most diplomatically Zavan thus speaks)

Zavan: As you wish sire …
though I do not wish a doomsayer to appear,
for I know how the princess to your heart is most dear.
But the dream I fear,
portents her as being the cause
of your empire's fall.

Astyages: What utter nonsense! My dear little flower!
How could she ever betray her loving father?
Why do I ever summon you to listen to your blether!

Zavan: I am sorry sire …. However I can but state the truth
according to the facts presented before me.
I only have your interest at heart.

Astyages: Of course you do… thank you for your most elucidating art.
Now get out of my sight you useless flea!
Before I have you flogged, you charlatan.. uncouth!

Zavan: As you wish my liege.
(Zavan bows and makes a most hasty retreat)

Anger subsided,
Astyages deeply contemplated.
Though he did not wish before Zavan to concede,
His words did confirm what he already did feel.

Astyages: Can it really be true… my sweet Mandane will be the end of my rule?
What utter nonsense! She could never entertain such a thought so cruel.
She loves me dearly … am I getting paranoid in my old age!
How could I even think such a thing of my innocent babe?
(So the mighty king thinks)

Over the next few weeks Astyages' tosses and turns in his bed-chamber
without respite and begins to ponder,
as his sleep is constantly interrupted by the same reverie.
So he finally resolves to marry his daughter to a noble so worthy
yet who could never be in a position contemplate such doom.
But whom … ?
(He muses)
Astyages: Who would be a worthy match for your daughter Astyages?
I can't marry her to a member of my family
that would be tempting fate.
If I marry her within the Median nobility
they would prove a worthy mate
but then have a direct claim to my territories.

'O' curse the gods for leaving me bereft of a son!
O Marduk, with you I am forever done!

What about my vassals? …. Hyrcania?
No… an extremely rich and fertile state … Parthia?
A desert state, no their king is too uncouth for Mandane … Bactria?
No! far too rich and strong with its fierce warriors … Cappadocia?
Definitely no! It's far too large and wealthy.
Persis… a poor and rugged mountainous nation
but is it worthy of my darling Mandane's station.
Mmm.. Cambyses of Anshan.

Yes! it can only be Cambyses…
a handsome and noble ruler of great integrity
and more importantly monarch of an insignificant state with a small army
hardly a match for the great Median force so mighty
should the unlikely eventuality ever come to be.
A cautious man ..an unlikely challenge to my supremacy
amongst the vassal nobility.
Yes! Cambyses shall be a most suitable match,
freeing me of worries of plots that powerful suitors may hatch.

And as he, in his mind so resolve,
calm once again prevailed upon his soul.
Happy and content at his prudence and rationality
the following day he summons his beloved queen,
Aryenis a vision of aesthetic delight, with such grace and sagacity
to his side in his private chamber to discover how his plan she would deem.

Astyages: Come my dearest, let's take a little stroll
in the courtyard for it is such a beautiful summer's day,
just feast your eyes at the myriads of roses ablaze
(As he takes a breath of the air around)
mmmmm their scent is such intoxication.
Even the Babylonian King's senses would be impressed by such a fusion
of fragrance and colour …
undoubtedly a design, to the eyes to bewilder.

Aryenis: My dear you are too kind in your praise.
And indeed it is most a beautiful day,
worthy of such a beautiful gaze.
(Not knowing what to make of his sudden interest in the flora and praise)

Astyages: So how is Mandane, it has been quite some time
since I saw her?

Aryenis: She is fine – she spends most of her time
with her cousins - especially Ushtra.

Astyages: And Mandane .. how old is she?

Aryenis: 16 she shall soon be.

Astyages: A woman then, about the same age I married you my darling.
And …. this Ushtra do you think he has of Mandane become desiring?

Aryenis: No, I think not …. They've always played together.

Astyages: In a brotherly manner?

Aryenis: Yes only in a brotherly manner.

Astyages: And is there anyone who does not look at her as a sister?
After all she is as enchanting and beautiful as her mother…
and she is without doubt an empyrean wonder.

Aryenis: My Lord does know how to flatter.
(She blushingly smiles)
Although… I have seen Prince Deioces paying more attention of late.
He has accompanied Mandane on several occasions to the market place.

Astyages: Has he? *(As a mischievous smile pervades his face)*
Well it is only natural that noticed by him and others she should be.
Tell me Aryenis – do you remember the Persian Cambyses …?

Aryenis: Cambyses of Anshan? Yes I do indeed…
he was a most polite and handsome young soul.
A pleasure to converse with… definitely not a noble bore!

Astyages: Well, I have given this matter some deliberation.

Aryenis: Have you now dear …And what matter has occupied your reflection?
**As a rather worrisome expression
prevails upon her heavenly disposition
as she tries to guess her husband's intention
for she had never known Astyages to bring up a topic of conversation
without careful deliberation**

Astyages: Mandane's marriage … and I have come to a decision …
she is to marry Cambyses, for he is the best match in my estimation.

Aryenis: Cambyses! …But my dear he is the regent of a small insignificant nation
don't you think your family will be angered if you gave her to someone foreign?
(As she tries calmly to discern the reason behind his choice)

Astyages: To hell with all those minions!
Waiting in the wings for my death to take over my dominions!
I couldn't care less about their covetous opinions!

Aryenis: But my darling, Anshan is so far away.
And though Cambyses is the most noble of your vassalry,
in Media we have many lowly courtiers richer than he.
My poor Mandane will find it so difficult to stay.

Astyages: She will be fine, Cambyses is a good soul;
he will look after her well or face Astyages' rage,
imprisoned in an iron cage.
Do not worry deprived she will be of nothing for I shall provide for all.

Aryenis: And have you informed Cambyses of your decision?

Astyages: I don't see any reason as to why I should seek his approbation.

Aryenis: Well, he may already be betrothed to some relation.

Astyages: Well, he will just have to UNBETROTH himself!
Who could be more worthy then the daughter of the mightiest king!
Any other will just have to become his concubine.
I shall summon Cambyses I am sure he shall be more then fine
when he learns of his good fortune he shall with joy sing.
Well I leave it to you then to inform Mandane to prepare herself.

**And so it came to pass that Cambyses of Anshan reluctantly did acquiesce,
knowing well the violent consequences of a refusal and wedded the Princess,
in all royal pomp and ceremony the like of which had not before been seen
to Cambyses and Mandane's delight love and devotion blossomed so keen.**

**A year passes and Astyages' sleep is once more disturbed by a recurrent vision
he sees a vine springing forth from his daughter
which comes to cover the whole of Asia.
So once again he summons Zavan to his displeasure,
To see if any words of consolation he could offer,
which may alleviate a fatal decision.**

Zavan: Greetings My Lord.
I trust you are well, for you exude resplendence?
How may this humble servant be of service to his glorious king?

Astyages: I am so joyous Zavan that I am just about to sing
as I see before me my saviour come to my assistance!
(Sarcasm to the extreme)
Magi - I am troubled by my old dream once more.

Zavan: I take it the Princess Mandane has appeared in your dreams again.

Astyages: Yes she has - my most perceptive brain.

Zavan: Well sire, if it is similar,
then I am afraid it portents the same danger.

Astyages: Yes it is similar, but how could that be possible?
Cambyses is neither strong enough nor has the inclination to me dare.
His forces are too weak in number to threaten my power!

Zavan: Well sire, though it may appear impossible…
but what if she a male child did bear
being your blood his claim on your throne would not be of a stranger.

Astyages: What am I to do, I cannot my own child murder.
She is what I above all treasure.

Zavan: Yes, sire but her child you could dispose;
otherwise great loss, he will you cause.
Astyages: Yes, Zavan but how could that be brought to pass
for when she is with child she shall be with Cambyses in Anshan.

Zavan: Median magi physicians are the best without any to surpass.
An anxious father worried about his daughter's health could call her to Ecbatan.

Astyages: You old dog – It has been a long while
since you have offered me advice of such guile.
(He evilly smiles)

Zavan: As I said my lord I am here to serve your desire.

Astyages: Well speak of this to no one or you'll experience my wrath and anger!
(Zavan bows his head and makes for a speedy retreat)

Part II
590 BC - Cyrus' Birth

And when Mandane was with child,
Astyages under the concerned father's guise
to Ecbatan summoned his daughter
to receive the best care Media had to offer.
Cambyses reluctantly agreed for he knew his physicians
were no match for Media's magi surgeons.

On Mandane's arrival, Zavan her personal physician became,
for he knew what had to be done,
in case she gave birth to a boy!
During the latter weeks of her pregnancy
Mandane was fatigued greatly.
Out of exhaustion she fainted giving birth to a boy.
Zavan, to Astyages presented him his grandson
who when he saw the beautiful babe remorse almost overcame.

All were told the child had died at birth
And Astyages who before was in great mirth,
was so utterly grieved
that he took the child to the mourning chamber
and had it buried.
Poor Mandane when she came round fell in a mood most sombre,
And hurried back to Cambyses in distress and shame,
who though in equal pain did his best to alleviate her anguish all the same
However, the truth was so,
when Cyrus the babe Astyages saw,
Astyages had Prince Harpagus the most loyal of his nobles beckoned,
and who without a hint of the morbid task at hand came as summoned.

Astyages: Tell me Harpagus how am I to know of your true loyalty?
How am I to be assured of your utter fidelity?

Harpagus: My Lord, you know there is nothing I would not do for your majesty.
You have been extremely gracious and have favoured me above all
I owe my wealth and position to you sire.

Astyages: Yes Harpagus I believe you probably would do anything for me.
However your lord will entrust a most wicked act to test your resolve
and should you betray his confidence will bring upon him a destruction most dire.

16

Harpagus: Sire, I am yours to command as you see fit,
your unswerving slave who would never question your design
or do anything that would bring harm upon your illustrious name.

Astyages: Then do as I say for it concerns the annihilation of my reign.
Take this grandson of mine,
and dispose of him - I insist!

Harpagus: My lord your humble slave has never before you disobeyed,
pray are you quite sure that there is no other course
then to have this child slain.

Astyages: Harpagus, it is my wish and needs to be obeyed.
I have given this much thought and there is no other recourse
the reasons as to why, shall secret to me remain.

Harpagus: Well, sire if that is your final word and demand,
then it will be carried out most diligently according to your command.

So the child wrapped in garbs of death, Harpagus took.
He hurried home and bolted the doors quickly.
His wife Humaya curious at the small bundle to look
thus asked Harpagus to see:

Humaya: What have you there hidden?
Why the anxious expression - what has HE ordered?

Harpagus: That madman has this babe me given
…his grandson and has commanded me to have him murdered.

Humaya: My darling, that man is truly without heart – but why?
What has this poor innocent done to justify such a heinous proclamation?

Harpagus: The tyrant gave no reasons as to why this child is to die.
But somehow he believes this babe linked, to his future destruction.

Humaya: What are we to do? …To kill such innocence would be the ultimate sin!

Harpagus: I haven't a clue. But I will not be responsible for killing my own kin.

Humaya: Astyages is an old man without a male successor,
if he should die and his daughter Mandane become ruler
whose son you are commanded to slay,
and were ever to discover... what of us then?

Harpagus: For our safety the child must be killed but by some other.
I do not wish to carry out this murder!
Let someone belonging to Astyages commit this crime without delay...
But who? ... Where? ... And when?

**And so, lost was Harpagus in deep rumination, til finally a name...
Mitradates! A Lydian herdsman in charge of the King's farm
situated in the mountains to the north of Ecbatan.
A rugged land covered by forest, and beasts roaming wild
populated with a few souls - a perfect place to dispose of the child
without leaving a trace.
This herdsman with extreme haste
on Harpagus' summoning came.**

Mitradates: I came as quickly as I could My Lord.
How may a humble herdsman be of service to your princely self?

Harpagus: You are to take this child yourself,
And have disposed by the beasts in the remotest part for some gold.

Mitradates: Yes My Lord, I shall do as you command.

Harpagus: Proof shall I require of your action
and should you fail or feign,
I promise suffer will you excruciating pain
as retribution!

Mitradates: Yes My Lord, I shall do as you demand.
(He speaks in a fearful tremble)

**And so the herdsman terrified took the child
and returned home under the cover of the obsidian night.
On arrival he found his wife Cyno, quite distressed,
and most depressed.**

Cyno: What was the extreme haste?
What did Harpagus want that could not wait?

Mitradates: I am afraid I have been entrusted with his heinous will.
On arrival at his place I was given this babe to kill.
(Showing the little child wrapped in a silken cloth of the most beautiful hues)

I was ordered by him to take this poor child and in the deepest forest to place
for the wild beasts to feed.
Refusal to carry out this murderous deed
will entail suffering a most painful fate.

And so Mitradates gave the child to his wife
who uncovered a most gorgeous babe
on seeing the child looking back with such a loving gaze
she burst into tears imploring her husband not to take such a blameless life.

Cyno: Mitradates I beseech you do not slay
this defenceless babe.

Mitradates: I have no choice, a horrid death awaits me if I falter
Harpagus requires proof of his order.

Cyno: If that's so, then take this still born child of ours who wasn't meant
(As trickles of sadness gently fell down her cheeks)
and expose it to the wild
and pretend it was this beautiful child.
No-one the truth shall discover;
so let's bring him up as if he was our,
for he surely is a gift from the Almighty Zeus sent!

Mitradates with eyes welled on hearing about the loss of his infant
accepted the advice of his imploring sable.
They wrapped their stillborn child in the garments silken
and lay it in a cradle.
He took his dead child in the forest deep
and tied the cradle to a tree,
leaving it there for days numbering three.
On returning a blood splattered cradle with a few bones did he see
and did weep.
This as evidence to Harpagus he brought,
who seeing the blood stains and bones, proof no more sought.

Part III
Cyrus' Childhood

So it was that the young Cyrus was brought up by the couple most happy.
A handsome intelligent and upright child he grew to be,
helping his father with the chores of the farm.
The proud parents doted upon him captivated by his loving charm.
Loved by all the children he was carefree.
But Cyrus' idyllic life as the herds-boy Kasra ended suddenly.

In Cyrus' tenth year Prince Artembares, Astyages relation
came to the farm for an inspection,
accompanied by Sama his son who was spoilt and proud.
Cyrus was playing with his friends when Sama came to join the little crowd

Franya: I nominate Cyrus as King to us lead.

All the children: We all agree.

Cyrus: Thank you my faithful lot.
Right Araxa, Byarshan, you are to construct me a fort
and I wish it to be the best and most awe inspiring stronghold.

Araxa/ Byarshan: Yes your majesty.
(They all laugh)

Cyrus: Dratha, Erexsha being the strongest, shall have the honour of guarding me!

Dratha/ Erexsha: Thank you for entrusting us such a demand.
We are at your service, to do as you command.
(They all laugh jokingly)

Cyrus: And you Franya my friend being the most intelligent soul
(Laugh Cyrus and all and say: Him intelligent even the goats have more sense)
shall be my right-hand confidant trusted above all.

Sama: You herds-boy, I am Prince Sama and shall be the king!
(Pointing to Cyrus)
Cyrus: General in command you can be for I am already chosen a king!

Sama: Me general! Being a prince, to be king is my prerogative to demand!
How dare a peasant boy be king in my royal presence!
Cyrus: A prince you are indeed and honoured I have your noble attendance.
But here I am chosen king, so obey must you my command!

Sama: How can a lowly goatherd order a prince - such impudence!

Cyrus: Guards seize that boy and tie him up for his insolence!
(Dratha and Erexsha seize Sama and tie him up while as he struggles and protests)

Sama: Let me go! How dare you lay, your filthy hands upon my princely being!

Cyrus: Enough of your impertinence shut up or suffer a right royal beating!

Sama: You are no king but a peasant, a coward and a fraudster,
untie me and I shall teach you a lesson with my fists that you will remember!
*(In a commanding and confident tone did he speak
being much older and bigger than Cyrus whom he viewed weak)*

Cyrus: Is that so prince? …Though you be confident of your strength and are older,
you shall pay for your rude and ill manner!

Dratha, Erexsha! Untie this impudent PRINCELY Sama!

**Sama untied, immediately lunged for Cyrus
But he was too agile and evaded his blow.
Cyrus riposted with his own knockout blow
on Sama's chin who fell with a thud to the floor,
Cyrus pinned him down and started punching more
until the boy started crying and so stopped Cyrus.**

Cyrus: So you admit defeat?

Sama: Yes, stop please!
(Sobs he)

**Cyrus let the boy go and he ran to his father
informing him of what had taken place.
Artembares furious with such effrontery could not contain his anger
and chastised Mitradates to his face.**

Artembares: Goatherd! How dare your cur attack his superior!
Have you taught him no reverence?
Mitradates: My Lord forgive him his lack of deference,
he is only a child who did not realise his error.

21

Artembares: Forgive him I shall **NOT** wait till I inform the King of such brazen
disrespect.

Mitradates: I beg of you my most gracious lord- pardon his inadvertent
lack of respect.

Artembares: Worthless creature - get out of my sight!
And await your painful plight!

**Artembares complained to the King who for the sake of family displeasure
summoned Mitradates and his son before him to measure.
Cyrus entered with head high while Mitradates, cowered head low.
Astyages fixed his eyes upon the two and then spoke to Cyrus so:**

Astyages: How does a lowly goatherd deem fit to visit violence upon royalty?
Do peasants dare show such contempt to their nobles with utter disloyalty!

Cyrus: My Lord, I treated him with the respect that he deserved.
I was chosen king by the boys of my village who deemed me the most worthy.
I appointed him my general but he refused and wished to be king.
He challenged me, so he received what he deserved.
Beaten was in fair combat as I proved myself worthy.
If you deem my actions wrong then submit shall I to the will of my king.

**Astyages was struck by the cool and calm nature of this peasant spawn,
not the least overawed to stand before such a mighty emperor,
unlike his father who had the look of servile terror,
of a man out of place and mentally gone.
Enchanted by the boy's manner and eloquence,
and being a man most astute he wondered
how one so noble could of so lowly an origin emanate.
To uncover the truth of how such a boy came to originate,
he a while pondered,
and sought to examine Mitradates in Artembares and the boy's absence.**

Astyages: Artembares, I promise to resolve the manner to your satisfaction.
Now be gone and leave me to my interrogation!

Artembares: Yes sire, I shall leave it to your judicious deliberation.

**Not wishing to anger one so erratic in manner
he bowed and left his unpredictable master**

Part IV
The Truth Revealed

**Astyages signalled his attendants to lead Cyrus into his inner chamber,
so he could threaten Mitradates to speak of the boy's true nature.**

Astyages: Now listen herdsman and listen carefully
if you wish to leave here alive.
Tell me the origins of the boy truthfully,
for if you continue to lie
a most horrific end shall you incur!
Who is the child's true father, you CUR?

Mitradates: I.. I amm ..m..m.y Lord, I do not q..q..quite understand ….
(He answered in a frightened stammer)

Astyages: So you do not qqqquite Understand!
(Cruelly mocking Mitradates' stammer)
LIAR! - That boy in no form or shape resembles such a wretch as you!
Mock my intelligence not, he is far too noble to be born of lowly you!

**Mitradates frightened, began trembling,
knowing it was no use lying,
and so began to relate his tale
fearing for his fate:**

Mitradates: Forgive me sire, but you are right he is not mine
the child was entrusted to me by Prince Harpagus to be killed ten years ago.
But my wife beseeched me not to do so.
And when I saw his smile I could not bring myself to commit such a crime.
Please forgive my disobedience sire,
I did not wish to question Prince Harpagus' desire,
but, I am a lowly farmer not a killer.

Astyages: Enough! I should really kill you right now for disobedience
but you are in luck I am in an exceedingly good temper
and as such I shall to you be clement.
I cannot abide lowly creatures begging for their worthless existence,
especially disloyal ones who should incur my displeasure.
Guards, get this worthless dog out of my sight before I stop being lenient!

And so Mitradates relieved to leave with his life,
was led away and then realised he had lost his only son,
gloom and dejection came to cloud his life,
as he reflected on the prospect of being without his beloved son.
Astyages wishing a second opinion summons his Chief Magi Zavan once again
and recounts his predicament to see if his counsel may be to his gain.

Astyages: So what does my magi most wise propose this time,
for the gods have taken a shine to this grandchild of mine?

Zavan: Well my lord from what you of old described,
your dream the boy appears to have fulfilled.
For king was he chosen by the village children, his peers
and ruled over them like a king without any fears.
Commanded respect did he, punishing disobedience
therefore I bid you be happy for the inadvertent non-compliance.
For you have gained a grandson who will remove the cloud of sorrow
from your daughter, so hasten with the happy news that she may receive tomorrow.
Banish, further any fears of your kingdom's annihilation
And inform the world of your immense jubilation.
Inform all of the events so:
Say a loyal servant on hearing the king's vision
fearing the king's destruction,
in good faith had Cyrus removed at birth and sent to a distant habitation.
And now the gods have seen fit to remedy the unjust situation.
Worry not for many dreams turn out to have an interpretation less significant.

Astyages: Yes Zavan, I have often found your interpretations rather insignificant!

Zavan: Sire, I can but interpret what I see,
however the future is in constant flux
not forever set in sand and oft is affected by many an action.
We the magi are but interested in your well-being and happiness.

Astyages: Yes, I'm sure you are most interested in my well-being and cheerfulness.
You like most of my kin do not for me possess the slightest affection
And would deem it good luck,
to see the end of me – so off with you - LEAVE!

Zavan: As you wish sire.

Astyages: Yes that is my desire!
(Pleased at what he had heard Astyages summoned Cyrus)
Astyages: My dear boy, it appears a great wrong was done to you long ago.

Cyrus: My lord … how can that be so?

Astyages: My dear boy you are no herdsman's son
but my very own long lost grandson
for when you were born, a dream was wrongly interpreted
that mistakenly portended
you to be the end of me
and so out of misguided loyalty
a servant of mine unbeknown to me
in good faith had you removed from your royal family
and sent to the herdsman you call father to look after.
But all now is well for returned are you now to your real grandfather
and this day have I sent a message of your return to your father
King Cambyses of Anshan and your mother Mandane my daughter.

Cyrus: Thank you my lord, you are most grateful but of my mother and father?

**Cyrus inquired, in his calm and composed nature
unruffled at the tumultuous events that had changed his life forever**

Astyages: Forget them now and that life forever,
for you are Cyrus a prince and a herdsman no longer.

**Astyages for a moment contemplates whether leaving Cyrus living
was indeed a good plan as he observed with admiration
this child who stood so tall in his presence
may one day become a menace to his imperial existence.**

O Astyages do not unnecessarily vex.
Enough of your cowardly worry!
An emperor you are most mighty,
so stop being cast under an evil hex.
Of this miracle be happy
and question not its coming to be!

Astyages: Well my boy, to have you back, returned I am most joyous,
tomorrow I shall hold a banquet to mark this occasion most wondrous.

Guards, house Prince Cyrus in our guest quarters
and then summon Prince Harpagus
to me.
Immediately!
*(Cyrus is led to his new quarters. Harpagus arrives with all due haste
as commanded directly)*

Harpagus: What is it sire, how may I be of service?

Astyages: Sire, is it now – more like how may I be of disservice!

Harpagus: I do not understand… my Lord?

Astyages: Shut up! You my most trusted and loyal standard I thought,
are like all… a deceitful unworthy liar!

Harpagus: But, Sire me a deceitful ……. liar
(So pleads Harpagus)

Astyages: Do you not remember the task that I entrusted to you ten years ago? Traitor!
The boy is still alive! How could you have betrayed my confidence so?

Harpagus: The boy alive? That cannot be so sire,
for when you did trust me with that grave assignment
I resolved to carry it out as you commanded.
But though not wanting to be disloyal could not bring myself to kill the infant
who after all was my blood relation.
So without wishing to harm you in any way,
I thought it best to send the child far away.
To a herdsman I commanded to dispose the boy with utmost discretion
I threatened to have him killed if he disobeyed – that lying miscreant!
He showed me evidence of the child's death as demanded.
As I have failed you sire I shall willingly accept whatever punishment.
But my disobedience was not due to any malevolent desire.

**Thus Harpagus related the story and resigned himself to his mortal fate,
for Astyages the Tyrant was not given to merciful debate.**

Astyages: Yes, the boy is alive and I am most relieved
for I could no-longer bear the pain and penitence
of my sweet Mandane, so count yourself fortunate indeed
that I do not have you executed for your disobedience.
Now go! And tomorrow bring your son with you
for he shall become Cyrus' companion,
and to mark this miraculous occasion
a royal banquet shall I hold to introduce Cyrus for all to view.

Harpagus: Thank you my Lord for your gracious mercy,
for I deserved your wrath not kindness and generosity.

**Harpagus overjoyed with such a turn of event
for he was to be a guest rather than experiencing a cleft head.
He thanked the gods for his good fortune heaven sent.
So off home, happy he sped.**

Harpagus: Humaya praise Marduk, for your husband's had a lucky escape.

Humaya: A lucky escape?

Harpagus: Well you will never believe… that child I was commanded
by Astyages long ago to dispose ….

Humaya: Yes what of that poor child may Marduk bless his innocent soul.

Harpagus: Well the herdsman I entrusted to kill the child disobeyed my command
And brought up the child instead as his own.. that child is at present in the palace.
He summoned me to punish for not carrying out his demand,
but changed his mind and bears me no malice,
as he was overjoyed to see him alive.
Thank the empyrean gods for protecting us, from his evil eye.

Humaya: Oh my darling, praise indeed be to the gods, so gracious
for saving you from his nature so capricious.

Harpagus: And what's more our son is to be the boy's companion.

Humaya: O Harpagus… Providence has indeed bestowed on us its compassion.

The palace and the city were soon rife with rumour and suspicion.
A peasant boy from nowhere being paraded as Astyages grandson –
What games was that old fool playing?
What was its significance, its true meaning?
The nobles and all tried to guess Astyages' scheming.
For he was renowned for his astucious nature,
he revelled in causing uncertainty and fear.
Is this one of his trials to test our loyalty? They did ponder,
little realising that the peasant boy was Cyrus indeed.
And for the first time there was no scheming behind the thought of Astyages
for he was genuinely glad, his grandson to see.

Early next morning went Harpagus and son,
dressed in the finest garments to meet the king and his grandson.
Harpagus' son a handsome youth of twelve
was excited at such a prospect,
to see Cyrus and the King!
Little realising the evil nature of this meeting!
When they arrived, Astyages had Harpagus' son taken aside and slain,
cut into small pieces and cooked and served to his father at the feast.
A most wicked smile his evil face pervade, as happy to see the boy he did feign
Such vengeful deceit that only a malevolent beast could ever conceive.

Later at the banquet in the evening
Astyages bade Harpagus a welcome like never before.
Poor Harpagus little suspecting,
of what sorrow was soon to endure.

Astyages: Come Harpagus my friend sit to my right
I have laid a special table for you with the finest meats, drink and more.
(A smile unnervingly warm in welcome)
Harpagus: Sire without doubt you are without doubt a most gracious lord,
so forgiving and upright.

Astyages: Indeed I am Harpagus …
(He grins)
And this is my grandson Cyrus.

Harpagus: Good evening Prince Cyrus.
It is a pleasure to meet you.
(He warmly smiles)

Cyrus: Good evening Lord Harpagus.
It is a pleasure to meet you too.
*(Cyrus smiles awkwardly,
at what he sees as a gentle figure of great nobility
lost as he was in the royal surroundings of opulence, luxury
and all things aplenty)*

**Harpagus impressed by Cyrus' calm and noble stature,
feels extremely happy that the babe he did not slaughter.
So he sits down and eats his repast to his heart's content,
innocently unaware of Astyages' glee and fiendish intent**

Astyages: I see Harpagus the meal was to your satisfaction?

Harpagus: Yes sire, most appetising, the cook deserves great commendation.

Astyages: I shall pass on your appreciation.
I had him prepare a special meat in your praise.
Would you like to know its tender ingredient?
(He inquires gloatingly)

Harpagus: Yes sire, for I've never before tasted such a delicious creation,
I am sure it would be to Humaya's taste.
She will be fascinated to learn of its delectable element.

**Astyages commanded one of his guards to bring forth a creel
that contained Harpagus' son's head, hands and feet
and presented to the unsuspecting father
for Astyages vile pleasure.**

Astyages: You make take what you wish as a special gift from me.

**Harpagus, uncovered the basket to his horror,
for his precious son's remains did he uncover.
But composed he stayed
not wishing Astyages to delight in his pain,
like a true officer unfazed
did he remain.**

Astyages: Can you guess upon which beast's flesh you did feed?

Harpagus: Yes sire, I can indeed.

Astyages: And what do you make of the affair.

Harpagus: Whatever my lord resolves in his wisdom is always fair.

Forgive me my lord but I beg your leave for early tomorrow morning,
I am to inspect the troops and their combat training.

**Astyages waved Harpagus to be excused,
taking his son's remains he swore one day he'd be avenged!**

Part V
Cyrus Reunited With His Parents

**And so it was that Cyrus a few weeks later
was reunited with his parents most anxious
but also most joyous
unable to believe the greatest miracle ever**

*(At the palace in Anshan Mandane and Cambyses wait nervously
for this boy that was Cyrus... supposedly.)*

Mandane: O Cambyses can this really be true?
Could this boy really be ours – 'O' I so wish to be his mother.

Cambyses: Patience my darling we can but hope it to be true.
Even your father, would not conjure such a cruel trick upon his daughter.

Mandane: Oh Cambyses my heart will surely explode.
My very being trembles with excitement, if he is not ours I will implode!
(Suddenly outside there is great commotion)

Mandane: What's all that noise? Can it be he has arrived?

Cambyses: Wait here Mandane and I shall see what has transpired.

**Cambyses leaves the inner confines of his palace in great haste
with anticipation and heart pumping fast he goes to investigate**

Cambyses: Rostam what's all the excitement?

Rostam: My lord they are arrived to great cheer and enthusiasm.

**The streets were packed with people who had heard of Cyrus' coming,
and had all rushed to see him on his home coming.
The gates to the palace were cast open wide
to warmly welcome Cyrus and his escorts in perfect stride**

Cambyses: Welcome my friends of old.

Captain Bahador: Greetings my lord

Cambyses: I trust your journey was without great incidence?

Bahador: Yes sire – it was without any ill occurrence.

Cambyses: And this must be Cyrus?

**As he gazed upon Cyrus, he was struck by the serene expression
on this handsome child's face and smiled at him with great affection**

Bahador: Yes sire, this is Prince Cyrus.

Cambyses: Welcome Cyrus, to our humble city.
(shaking the boys hand firmly)

Cyrus: Thank you majesty.
(Cyrus greets his father in a nervous tone)

Cambyses: Come let us eat for you must all be hungry
after such a long journey.

**And so Cambyses to the dining hall led the company.
Meanwhile, Mandane beside herself waited impatiently.**

**Cambyses could barely eat as his gaze upon Cyrus was firmly fixed
who looked uneasy and ate a small amount,
some rice and a cup of water did he consume,
whilst the rest of the company heartily did consume
all the dishes and wine presented before them to the full amount.
Enchanted by Cyrus's noble manner, Cambyses' gaze remained fixed**

My nose and eyes... and Mandane's sweet face and curly locks so silky fine
Is he really mine…..?
(Cambyses thinks)

**And finally after what to Cyrus seemed a life-time,
all had had their fill and it was resting time**

Cambyses: Captain Rostam please show each guest to his chamber
they must be tired after their long journey in the afternoon swelter.

Rostam: Yes sire.

Cambyses: Now my friends its time for your relaxation
and again tonight we shall meet for meal and conversation.

Bahador: Thank you sire.

Cambyses: Right Cyrus, I think it is time we introduced you to one other
who has been waiting most anxiously - your mother.

Cyrus: Yes sire

Cambyses: Well my boy you may dispense with Sire and may call me father

Cyrus: Yes sire …. father.

**And so Cambyses leads Cyrus to his personal quarter,
where awaited nervously Mandane, his MOTHER.**

Mandane: Oh my darling Cyrus– I've been waiting so anxiously for you.
(She rushes forward to hug and kiss him all over)
I cannot believe my eyes – my darling is it really you.
How are you? How was the journey?
You must be tired and sleepy?

Poor Cyrus bombarded with so many questions, which to respond to first...

Cyrus: I am fine My Lady, our passage passed quickly.
We often rested so I'm not the least bit weary.

Mandane: Oh Cambyses did you ever hear such eloquent expression
and look at those piercing blue eyes and nose so prominent,
O Cambyses he is a mirror image of a young you.

Cambyses: Yes my darling, such articulation
at so tender an age worthy of a noble eminent
and regard his dark curly locks and oval face a perfect image of you.

And so the parents continued admiring their son lovingly,
while poor Cyrus disorientated and new
missed greatly his previous life that was carefree.
But mature beyond his age knew
that that life was forever gone,
and that Anshan was to be his home from now on.
The next few weeks Mandane kept her son ever near
like a woman living in permanent fear
of losing her beloved son so dear
she could not bare Cyrus out of sight nor tire of his voice to hear.

Part VI
Cyrus' Education In Anshan

In Anshan Cyrus received a moral education,
which was prized above all in Persian tradition,
At an early age the boys were instilled with ethical instruction:
The importance of treating all with respect and deference,
Holding their elders and superiors in reverence.
Shame and banishment, the ultimate punishment for transgression
Etiquette and decorum was of great import to the Persian
To spit, blow one's nose or give to flatulence was quite an indiscretion.

The education of the Persians was divided into phases four –
those of the *boys, youths, adults mature,*
and *Elders* of military service age no more.

The Boys - were taught the path to righteousness
of doing good and refraining from indulging in wickedness;
trained by their tutors to decide criminal cases involving their peers
Any boy accused of an offence was brought before his peers
to be tried and punished for culpable behaviour.
Crimes especially detestable to The Persian's demeanour
concerned false accusation and ingratitude -
The gods, family, friends and one's country behoved gratitude.

The importance of *self-control and self-restraint* was imbued
in the boys from the very beginning.
Moderation they endured in eating and drinking -
bread from home with some cress as relish did they bring
and a cup to fill from the river to quench their thirstful craving.
Learnt they also to shoot and hurl the javelin with deadly targeting.
Once they satisfied their teachers' standards most exacting
to the ranks of the young men at 16 and 17 they moved.

The Young Men -
For ten years the young men's duty was guarding
the government buildings at night and increase their sense of alertness
And when called for were at the government's disposal in the day too.
The king often took half his garrison when he went hunting
including some of the *young men*, to hone their skilfulness
in archery, not forgetting how to aim the spear true.

34

In addition, in the hunt they carried a sheathed sabre
and a light shield in case of a hostile encounter.

Hunting the Persians used as training to ameliorate
the soldiers' military skills and of endurance and sufferance.
On long chases after their hunt, they would haste,
experiencing hunger and thirst, frore and incalescence.

Meagre provisions for one day's luncheon would they take,
bread and cress or any game killed for relish
became supper when the chase did not early finish
and so they would hunt again the following wake.

The young men who remained home, in constant training
were engaged in javelin hurling,
hand-to-hand combat and archery.
Competed, they in contests to perfect their proficiency
Prize and honour was bestowed on those displaying the greatest ability;
And those who exhibited the most discipline in drilling;
And the officers in charge of the training
were honoured with position and promotion,
that merited their command and instruction.
Others were employed in policing the city
ensuring order was maintained and punished any form of criminality.

After ten years of service as *young men*
they were promoted to the ranks of - **Mature Men**
For twenty-five years more service to their nation.
Trained they to ranks of the military men in addition
Clothed for close combat in a corselet which on their breast rested,
with a round shield on the left arm,
and a sabre in their right-hand, ever ready to inflict on enemy harm
And from this class of men were the magistrates also selected.

And when the *mature men* attained age fifty
took their place among the **Elders**, inveighed with great responsibility,
elected did they officers and officials of the kingdom,
and dealt with all private and public cases in the dominion.
Guardians of Persian Law were they
all appeals to any judgment came their way.

And so the Persians grew to be a fearless and robust nation,
brought up on a moral and physical diet of moderation.

Cyrus being ten was enrolled to the ranks of the *young boys*
He excelled in his moral, physical and military education.
A most competitive child with hard practice, toil and graft
sought always to better himself in whatever event he took part.
Humble in victory or defeat, held was he in the highest estimation
for his hard work, amongst his tutors and other young boys.

By the time Cyrus was promoted to the ranks of the young men
He had grown to be a most bright noble and handsomest of young men.

Part VII
Cyrus' Return To Ecbatan

Astyages longing to see Cyrus had him summoned
with his mother to his royal court.
Cyrus was most pleased to see his grandfather most imperially adorned,
as he was in his regal purple tunic and necklaces and bracelets of gold.
A wig of false hair with pencillings beneath his eyes and on his face rouge
porting silver and gold threaded leather shoes,
greeted Astyages his upright and handsome grandson lovingly.
Cyrus gazed at his grandfather in all his majesty
hugged and kissed this imposing soul most affectionately.

Astyages: My dear boy how you have grown to a fine figure
most handsome and charming from what I hear.
I fear for the entire female nobility resident in my Media.
They will swoon with delight once they gaze upon you near.
(As he roars with laughter while Cyrus smiles most bashfully)

Cyrus: You are most kind sire.

Astyages: And extremely humble too,
well it will appear the ladies will have to do all the chasing with you.
Come sit beside me for a while, for soon we shall move to the dining hall
where you will experience a most sumptuous feast in your honour for all.

Cyrus: You should not have my lord – it is sufficient honour
that you summoned mother and I to your courtly splendour.

Astyages: Nonsense my boy, you are the grandson
of King Astyages and son of my beloved daughter.
Today all my royal vultures will see you and wish for a similar son
and be not so formal Cyrus and call me grandfather.

Cyrus: As you wish grandfather.

Astyages: That's better, now I'm speaking to my grandson not a stranger.
So how was your journey to Media?

Cyrus: It was quite uneventful through Persia.

However, ambushed were we down a narrow passageway
by a band of robbers last night
probably mistaking us for merchant's caravans and thought us easy prey.
But paid they a bloody price, some put to the sword while others took flight.

Astyages: How dare they attack my Cyrus and Mandane!
By Marduk when I discover their identity the whole village shall pay.
Captain! Inform Prince Gubaru to investigate this action most grave.
He's to exterminate the village for attacking the royal cavalcade

Cyrus: Surely grandfather it is unjust to punish the blameless
for the crimes of the guilty, for that would be wicked and senseless.

Astyages: My dear boy you have a lot to learn,
it will serve as a lesson for any future bandits never to make
an attack on a royal cavalcade even by mistake.
Such an attack by lowly creatures deserves punishment
most firm otherwise we will have the peasants rising above their station
and tomorrow a rebellion.
Fear my boy is the most important weapon for an emperor.
With terror obedience and allegiance come to the ruler.

**Cyrus realising his grandfather was not a man of morals like his father
thought it pointless to press the matter any further.**

Astyages: Come my boy, it is time for the feast,
a visual delight and veritable treat.
But no wait! So humbly garbed will not do for a prince of Media.
I've bought you new clothes worthy of your princely position here,
resting in your chambers
Artabazus! Take Prince Cyrus to his private quarters.

Artabazus: Yes my lord. Please follow me to your quarters Prince Cyrus.

Artabazus: I shall wait outside for you Prince Cyrus.

Cyrus: Thank you Captain Artabazus.

And so Cyrus was shown to his rooms, where on his bed lay
the most beautiful silken garments so gay,
and jewel encrusted golden bracelets so wondrous
and necklaces so dazzlingly marvellous.

Cyrus adorned in jewellery and a brilliant purple dress,
Shone like Polaris, the celestial North Star
– Cyrus how wonderful and regal you are -
he thought himself
But realising his narcissism
reproached his egotism:

Fool, by beautiful things how easily you are captivated!
What of all the self-restraint and temperance?
Your father would be so disappointed.
You have been here but a day yet already have lost sense.

(Cyrus leaves his quarters and opens the door)

Artabazus: Most handsome you look Prince Cyrus
all gazes especially of the ladies shall be upon you.

Cyrus: Thank you Captain Artabazus.
(Smiles Cyrus bashfully)
You are too kind, I am sure many a lady's gaze on you aim so true

Artabazus: Sadly no more, as married am I most happy
(He jokingly smiles)

Cyrus: Well a lady most lucky must your wife be.

As they neared the hall, Cyrus could hear noise of courtly parlance,
and when he was announced, there was deadly silence.

39

Part VIII
The Banquet

Announcer: My Lords, Ladies and Gentleman - Cyrus Prince of Anshan

All the gazes became transfixed on his heavenly presence
Even Astyages himself was awe struck at his magnificence.

Astyages: Come Cyrus… and sit beside us here!

Thus was the silence broken by Astyages – who was beaming with pride,
at Cyrus his graceful grandchild.

Cyrus: As you wish grandfather,
greetings mother dear and dearest grandmother.

Aryenis: My how handsome you look my dearest child.
You make me so full of pride.

Astyages: Yes isn't he just the most splendid one here,
in looks and demeanour without peer.

Aryenis: Without a doubt dear.

When Cyrus gazed upon the food laid before his sight,
it was a veritable visual delight,
dishes, sweet and savoury meats, sauces and fruit of all kind
did Prince Cyrus find.

Cyrus: My god grandfather it would appear your cooks
have cooked for a whole village.

Astyages: Indeed my boy, my nobles could eat for a whole village.
But don't you think a fine gastronomic spectacle it looks.

Cyrus: A delectable delight indeed grandfather
but you must remember us Persians in moderation do we eat,
Just enough to satiate our hunger and no more.

Astyages: That as maybe Cyrus but remember
you are half Mede after all, and we Medes love to eat,
Even though our stomachs may be fill we can always make room for more!

Cyrus smiled and not wishing to offend
tasted all the dishes till he had consumed more than his heart's content.

Astyages: So my boy, how do you like the taste
of all the dishes before your face?

Cyrus: They are most delicious but I fear if I eat anymore
my stomach shall surely explode.

Astyages: Mine too
(merrily drunk he roared with laughter)
and tomorrow I have another surprise for you.
(The banquet came to an end with Astyages and his wife Aryenis retiring)

Astyages: Well goodnight my boy and see you in the morning.

Aryenis: Good night my darling.

Cyrus: Goodnight grandfather.
Goodnight grandmother.

(Mandane asks Cyrus how he had enjoyed his grandfather's hospitality)
Mandane: So Cyrus what do you think of your grandfather's hospitality?

Cyrus: I enjoyed it greatly!
Grandfather has been most generous mother,
but I fear here I shall become extremely fat and lazy
if I have to eat so much for lunch and dinner.

Mandane: Don't worry my darling,
after all you could do with a little fattening
(she teases him)
and be even more handsome and stronger than you already are.
I am so proud of you my darling, you carried yourself most proper.
The gaze of the whole household was upon you as the star.

Cyrus: You do flatter me so mother.

Mandane: Most handsome your are irrespective of my bias as your mother

Cyrus: Well I do take after you and father,
and there is no-one more beautiful and enchanting as you,
nor more noble and handsome as father,
So you may say I was doomed to be as wonderful as both of you.
(They both smile like a loving mother and child)

Cyrus: Good night mother dear.

Mandane: Good night my treasure

Part IX
Astyages' Gift

And so mother and son parted to their private chambers.
In the morning having breakfasted Cyrus was escorted
by Captain Artabazus to the royal stables
there most pleased Astyages waited.

Astyages: Well my boy, I promised you a surprise last night.
Behold Atash[2], the swiftest and most elegant of my mares.

Cyrus overjoyed: saw before him the most beautiful snow-white mare,
he had ever seen with a gold-studded bridle that like the sun dazzled.
In his father's country there was no mare of such compare.
Persia was not conducive to breeding horses being a country most rugged.
As such his father only possessed two hundred in cavalry
formed of the illustrious elite royal guards of repute and gallantry.

Cyrus: Oh grandfather – this is the most beautiful and graceful of mares.
Thank you so much, what a magnificent sight!

Astyages: You are welcome my boy, we can't have a grandson of mine
without the most splendid horse in the kingdom.
Come, mount your steed so fine
and let's hunt in the park and have some fun!
I have all manner of game here
I am told you are a great shot with the arrow and spear.

Cyrus: Thank you grandfather, I'm not sure about a great shot though,
but I would love to ride Atash and see how he will in my reins go.

So Cyrus, Astyages and his guards bestrode their steeds
and so began the hunt, Cyrus spotted a dear
and on Atash like the wind was quickly upon its heels
and with an aim so true, shot it with his arrow for all to see clear.

---

[2] Fire

Astyages: My word Cyrus, what a great shot!
Even Harpagus would have been proud of such an aim
and he's the best amongst my men to emulate.
(Spoke Astyages most proudly)

Cyrus: Thank you grandfather, it was just a lucky shot,
In no way can I lay claim to having so true an aim
as Prince Harpagus whose prowess even my father's men try to emulate

Astyages: Nonsense my boy, do not be so humble in your feat!
For that was the shot of a true marksman indeed.

The company hunted for a few hours more
Even Astyages managed to spear a boar
or rather presented with an opportunity to do so by Artabazus' feign
who drove one towards Astyages to with his spear claim.

Artabazus: Bravo sire that was a great throw.

Cyrus: Well done grandfather that was a great kill.

Astyages: There is still life in the old devil, but for today no more,
My stomach is rumbling, so we must put an end to the thrill
(He smiles with great satisfaction
and so the company heads back to sate their starvation)

Cyrus was allowed to hunt as often as he wished –
With other princes of his age
loving the thrill of the chase
and any excuse to ride Atash his pride.
As his grandfather's kitchens of meat were plenty supplied,
amongst his friends he distributed many a game he killed

The boys spent much time competing and in military training,
Shooting, wrestling, hurling spears and running.
Though fiercely competitive, he was always humble in victory
and accepted defeat most graciously,
congratulating his friends for their performances.
Cyrus would practise even harder to overturn his losses.

Cyrus, knowing how hard boys his age practised back in Anshan
was loathed to fall behind so practised with Harpagus whilst in Ecbatan.
His work ethic and extreme loyalty
endeared him to his tutors and peers equally.
Praised and loved by all for his courage and modesty was he.

Part X
A Day At The Training Ground

Harpagus: Cyrus my boy you are the best cadet here, definitely!
I fear you will soon become a greater shot than me
and as for your hurling well you have made me your inferior.

Cyrus: No my lord, that is not true at hurling you are much the superior
and still a supreme shot without peer for all clearly to see
My improvements are due to your training entirely.

Anyhow my horsemanship is far poorer than yours and that is definitely true.

Harpagus: A matter of time Cyrus, before you are a supreme rider too

Cyrus: You are most kind in praise my Lord Harpagus.

Harpagus: Only if it is deserving… Cyrus.

Cyrus: Tell me Lord Harpagus, I have heard, for a hunt you are preparing
and early tomorrow morning you and some of your troops are leaving.

Harpagus: True indeed Cyrus, hunts outside the park are good training,
for maintaining one's military skills and their further honing.

Cyrus: Well Lord Harpagus …. I was just wondering
if there was any possibility of me riding along with you.
Back in Anshan, young men my age often go hunting.
(Cyrus asks sheepishly)

Harpagus: I am afraid Cyrus I cannot take you hunting
Lord Astyages would never allow such a thing of you.
It is far too dangerous in the wild so you may stop your wondering.

Cyrus: But it is no sport hunting in the park an enclosed space
where the animals are far too easy to see,
docile and domesticated they are such easy prey.

Harpagus: I am sorry Cyrus, but hunt must you in that place.
Imagine how your parents and grandfather would grieve,
if anything tragic to you happened here on your stay.

Cyrus, dejected and disappointed,
dropped his head and to his quarters retired.
That evening in his courtyard he and his friends rather forlorn
talked about the hunt that was to take place the following morn.

Cyrus: Wish we could go on the hunt it's no fun in the park anymore.
The animals are far too mangy and slow.
Confined to the park they have no escape, nor any desire to go.
It is like hunting animals caged forever more,
unlike the wild beasts roaming free in open space.
With gazelles so sleek and fast that they seem to dance on air
and boars so fierce and wild that they charge with such dare
like warriors possessed in mortal combat's face.

Tigranes: I know Cyrus – I have asked my father several times.
It is too dangerous, I am too young - he claims!

Araspas: True Tigranes – I have also asked my father many times
with the same response – too young, too dangerous - he maintains

Cyrus: So are our protestations doomed to fail?
Well gentlemen what arguments can we proffer in order to prevail?

Araspas: There is only one way,
somehow Cyrus you must convince Lord Astyages to consent
and then our fathers out of shame, will no excuses find.

Cyrus: I am afraid Lord Astyages is not given to changing his mind.
How am I to gain his assent?
He is so difficult to sway!

Tigranes: He is your grandfather so try guilt and emotional blackmail,
plead enough times and he will eventually give in without fail!

Cyrus: Well I shall try with emotional blackmail my grandfather to assail.

(Next evening Cyrus goes as promised to Astyages and so pleads)
Cyrus: Grandfather, I was wondering if I may possibly request a favour?

Astyages: You were wondering were you? So you desire a favour?

Astyages smiles remembering the words of his daughter,
whenever she wanted something disapproved of by her mother

Cyrus: Well grandfather – as you know I love hunting
however, the animals in the park are far too easy to chase,
So, I wondered if tomorrow with Prince Harpagus hunting I may go.
(Asking most sheepishly)

Astyages: Hunting with Harpagus you may not go!
Out of the question! It is far too dangerous for you to go on the chase.
How would I forgive myself if an accident to you befell whilst hunting?

Cyrus: But grandfather, I am great at shooting and hurling,
you said yourself and I have improved greatly at riding.

Astyages: Out of the question Cyrus – just imagine how your poor mother
and father would feel if injury or more you did suffer?
They would never forgive me,
nor I at my decision, remain happy.

**Knowing that Astyages was not one to change his mind
Cyrus admitted defeat and retired to his chambers gloomy.
However, after a few weeks Astyages seeing Cyrus extremely unhappy finally
relented as to make Cyrus happy a way he could not find.**

Part XI
The Hunt & Cyrus' Last Months In Ecbatan

Astyages: Dear child I can no-longer countenance such a sad Cyrus
so this Friday, hunting you may go with Harpagus.

Cyrus: Oh grandfather – truly you are the most generous king!
(And hugs and kissed he his grandfather, beaming with delight)
Just one thing grandfather could my friends with me come.

Astyages: I am afraid the princes are most protective of their off-spring.
They do not wish to lose their precious heirs to accidents – to sum.

Cyrus: But grandfather, how would it look if I your grandson
was allowed to go hunting and they could not come.
I am sure each would be more than happy to send his son
if to their embarrassment they discovered I amongst the young
was the only one.

Astyages: A clever young man you are Cyrus.
(Smiles Astyages)
I will let it be known that Cyrus will be going on the hunt with Harpagus
and any young princes wishing to come along would be most welcome,
that should embarrass them into letting their precious souls to come.

And so it was that Cyrus contrived for his friends to with him go.
Before the hunt Harpagus spoke to Cyrus and his young friends so:

Harpagus: Now boys pay attention do not forget what I say.
At all times are you to remain close to me and follow my way,
for there are many dangerous beasts that may kill you if you stray
and many a precarious and precipitous place you will encounter this day.

49

But Cyrus being young, brazen and daring,
as soon as he espied a gazelle gave chase with adrenalin pumping.
He rode Atash swift as the devil himself, almost being thrown clear
as Atash jumped high over some rocks near a cliff so sheer
he just managed to stay astride eventually drawing close for the spearing.
Overjoyed with his kill he was now ready to face a stern admonishing.

Harpagus rode beside Cyrus and him reprove.
Soon followed by Astyages in hot suit
who although quietly proud had to disapprove,
Cyrus' bravery and skill in pursuit.

Harpagus: And what did I say to you before the hunt Prince Cyrus?

Cyrus: To remain close to you Lord Harpagus.

Astyages: Then prey tell, why you disobeyed and nearly got yourself killed?

Cyrus: Sorry grandfather, Prince Harpagus but I could not help myself rushing
for seeing the gazelle, my heart started pumping.

Astyages: So thrilled that you nearly got yourself killed!

He smiles at Cyrus – recognizing himself in him - as many years before
on his first hunt he too had forgotten all the warnings of his father
and nearly had himself killed whilst chasing a boar,
so he understood well why Cyrus on his first wild hunt became so eager.

That evening Cyrus still excited with his great hunting skill
visited his mother to recount about his thrilling kill.

Cyrus: Oh mother you should have seen me ride,
Atash I rode like the wind with such pride …
I was the first to make a kill,
with such skill …

Mandane: I am sure you were wonderful my darling,
after all you take after your father
and there is no horseman in the whole of Anshan finer.
I am sure he would be greatly joyed at your daring.

But tell me Cyrus we have been here a year now in Ecbatan
don't you miss your father back in Anshan?

Cyrus: Of course I do mother but I cannot go without feeling disappointed.
In Anshan I am the best at using the bow and hurling the javelin
but here not quite so, and my riding is still below the level I expected.
Prince Harpagus is a great teacher and I wish to be as good as him.
In another six months I shall be ready to depart.
Before you know it, time will quickly fly past.

Mandane: But my darling what of your moral education?
You will hardly learn the virtues of justice being with your grandfather.
He rules with an iron fist, his will suffers no dissension.
He is the absolute master of his kingdom, unlike your father
who rules with consent of the people of his nation
and is not above the Persian Law in station.

Cyrus: Do not concern yourself with my moral education mother
I am well versed in the principles of justice and righteous behaviour...
I have Master Arsalan to thank for that, as he is a most wonderful tutor.
(He smiles)

Mandane: Oh ...so you have learnt ALL, *(she smiles)* from your master.

Cyrus: Well not all ... a year ago I decided a case between two boys.
An older boy had taken from a younger boy a tunic
which was too long for him and handed to the younger his own tunic
that was too short for him but a perfect fit for the younger of the boys.

I decided that the older boy should keep the tunic
which he had taken from the younger boy,
especially as the older boy had given him his tunic
which I reasoned to be an equal recompense for the younger boy,
as his own tunic was too long for him to wear.
So I thought no crime had been committed and deemed my judgment fair.

Master Arsalan being present gave me a right royal flogging
which I shall not forget easily;
for I overlooked the principle of ownership of property.
No person can claim right to someone else's belonging
especially if taken forcibly.
Even if the boy gave the younger his tunic it negated not his criminality.

Mandane: And rightly so, Cyrus – well let further punishment
be on your head if you miss out on your moral education;
for you if you fall behind in your ethical instruction
and again make similar errors of judgment
then you will justly deserve another good beating
from Master Arsalan's flogging.
(They both laugh)

Cyrus: That's quite alright mother,
I shall take my chances with Master Arsalan's examining,
but first I must improve my military training
so when I return I shall be the best even as a rider.

Mandane: If that is your wish then I shall leave you my darling
for extremely lonely has become your father.

Cyrus: Thank you mother,
for when I return more accomplished father will feel like celebrating.

Mandane: I am sure your father
on seeing you alone, will feel like merry making.

**Cyrus stayed for another six months often with Harpagus hunting
and perfecting his skills til he was almost his equal in riding.**

Harpagus: It would appear I can teach you no more Cyrus.
You are as good as me,
and will soon better me.
For a far better shot and rider you are than I at your age Cyrus.

Cyrus: Thank you most kind Lord Harpagus,
however my improvement is entirely your doing.
For you are without doubt an officer without peer in skill and training
and who I am fortunate to have as my instructor.

Harpagus: Thank you Cyrus – you certainly know how to flatter
(Smiles Harpagus with pride at Cyrus' compliments)

Though Cyrus enjoyed greatly his time in Ecbatan,
However, with his mother gone he increasingly yearned for Anshan.
For he became ever more aware of his grandfather's intemperateness
Astyages often drank to excess and in his state of drunkenness
punished those around him for the slightest contravention,
He had Artabazus whipped and held for a week in detention
because he was slightly delayed arriving when beckoned.
And the judgments that he rendered when petitioned
appeared to Cyrus to be without rhyme or reason.
If he liked the look of somebody's dress that was sufficient justification
for his adjudication
thus people at peril sought to him petition.

Once a couple of farmers requested Astyages ruling
over a piece of land which both claimed as theirs being.
Astyages seeing one dressed in red, the same colour as himself
Outraged was he... and to himself thought
how dare you dress yourself,
in the same colour as your Lord!
And gave judgment for the other farmer
while the one in red he had executed for his social error.
Such were the whimsical reasons behind his pronouncements.
Indeed he deliberately revelled in creating uncertainty with his judgements.
Cyrus began slowly to notice more what fear Astyages did inspire.
He could feel Astyages' pleasure in inflicting pain and terror.

Finally one Friday Cyrus his grandfather's permission requested
and to Anshan headed.

Cyrus: I am so grateful for all you have done for me grandfather
but as you know I must leave now, for impatiently await my father
and mother.

Astyages: Well I shall miss you greatly my boy and so will your grandmother.

Aryenis: It will be a lonely affair without you near,
so hurry soon back here.
(She wipes a tear from her eyes)

Cyrus: I promise to grandmother most dear
(and a few days later Cyrus was ready to leave)

Cyrus hugged and kissed Astyages and his grandmother
whom he had grown to deeply love and admire.
She was the epitome of grace, beauty and compassionate nature.

His friends and Harpagus to the city gate did Cyrus accompany,
for he had inspired great affection and amity
amongst his peers and teachers because of his loyalty and modesty.

**Cyrus gave many gifts that he had received from his grandfather
and others to his friends
such as a fine purple robe given to him by his grandfather
which he gave to Tigranes, a most faithful of friends.
And to Harpagus he gave a most beautiful bejewelled dagger
sheathed in a golden scabbard to thank this noble prince without peer.**

Part XII
Cyrus' Visit To His Foster Parents

On his stay in Ecbatan Cyrus often wished
to see his old friends and foster parents
but did not do so, not wishing to offend his mother
who had no desire to share his love with another,
especially with his foster parents
whom she never acknowledged
fearing them as rivals for Cyrus' affection.
So Cyrus did pass by his old home under the cloak of the aphotic night
leaving his guards a little behind and knocked on the door with trepidation.
The couple suddenly awoke from deep sleep with a fright
Mitradates went to investigate with a sword in hand held firmly
did from inside demand angrily:

Mitradates: Who goes there at such an ungodly hour!

Cyrus: Open up in the name of the emperor!

(Opening the door half asleep Mitradates encounters a young nobleman)
Mitradates: Come in my lord, how may we be of service to you?

Cyrus: I am ravenous, how about feeding me some of your rabbit stew?

**His favourite dish - he would often go hunting,
with his father for rabbits to bring back for stewing**

Cyno: Kasra! It's you my darling boy!
O how I have missed you so… for without you there has been no joy.
(Cyno cries as she rushes to hug and kiss her very son once more)

Mitradates: What are you doing woman?
How dare you touch a nobleman!

**Thus castigated Cyno embarrassed with her familiar way,
withdrew her loving embrace right away.**

Cyno: Sorry my lord, forgive this old fool, her familiar manner.

Cyrus: Do not worry mother dear,
for I shall always be Kasra to you and father.

**So, father and son sat conversing about many a hunting expedition
whilst mother frantically spread all the fruit she could muster
before him and started to cook her son's favourite stew.**

Cyno: My darling Kasra, it pleases me so
to gaze upon you once more.
That day when your father back came
without you most lonely and sad we became.

Mitradates: Your mother was most distraught,
and it was so hard to her console.
I myself lost and lonely became,
as my heart heavy with your loss did pain.

Cyno: This day we thought we would see never
when our boy... a prince... would come to us remember.

Cyrus: I have missed you both deeply,
all these years I have thought about you greatly,
and often wished to come this way,
but never had the occasion till this day.

Cyno: What a handsome young man you have grown to be.

Mitradates: Most definitely!

Cyrus: You are most kind mother ... father

Mitradates: A princely figure,
with a humble nature.

**They stayed up all night in deep conversation
Cyrus managed but a few hours slumber
and in the morning went to see the friends he once knew.**

**For his friends he brought gifts of many an arrow
and bow.
Friends reunited once more,
they conversed like yesteryears before.**

Cyrus: Is that you Dratha and Erexsha,
my trusted bodyguards of old?

Dratha: Indeed so.

Erexsha: We never thought we'd ever see you Kasra.

Cyrus: Well how could I not come and see my friends again.
And where is Franya, my confidant with the biggest brain?
(They all in jest smile)

Erexsha: Hiding behind Byarshan and Araxsha.
(Franya, shyly steps forward)

Cyrus: Shy as always Franya.

Franya: Yes, your Highness.
(Being the first to acknowledge Cyrus' true station)

Cyrus: You may dispense with Highness Franya,
to you my friends I am forever Kasra.

Cyrus: Well my friends I have brought a few things for you
to remind you of our friendship anew.
Remember how we used to make our own arrows
and bows
and practised our shooting.
Well here are the finest bows and arrows that I could bring.

Franya: You are most kind Kasra.

The Rest: Indeed you are!
(All most grateful and happy as they admire their gifts keenly)

Cyrus: It was my pleasure,
for to see my old friends most dear,
has made me most happy to be here.

Araxsha: So what's it like being a prince in Persia?

Cyrus: Easier than my life here in Media.
People who wait upon me wherever I go,
I live a life of luxury like you wouldn't believe so!
(He smiles sarcastically)

Byarshan: Wow… a life of luxury.
Can you take me with you?

Cyrus: Well… I would be more than happy to take you
provided you can wake up early,
and do two hours of rigorous military training, every morning,
followed by schooling in law and morality
and then more military training,
and yes not forgetting meals that we eat aplenty.
If you enjoy bread and cress for relish then I would be happy
to take you along with me.

Byarshan: On second thoughts, here I am more than happy,
living the life of a herdsman carefree.

Erexsha: Yes you were always the most hardworking,
you lazy being.
(They all laugh heartily)

**And so after a few days stay,
it was time for Cyrus to be on his way.
Out he brought gifts for his mother and father
and monies of gold and silver.**

Cyrus: Here mother dear
I have chosen for you the finest silken wear in the whole of Media.
And you father how could you in your old garments with mother go?
So I have bought clothes befitting your noble soul.

Cyno: You shouldn't have my dear,
seeing you was sufficient a gift for this poor woman.

Mitradates: Your mother is right Kasra, the fact that you are here
the hearts of this old couple gladden.

Cyrus: Nonsense, you will always be my parents
and that much will never change.
It pained me think that whilst I was enjoying my princely life
here toiled and struggled so my parents.
So here is a bag full of gold and silver coins to bring a renewed change
and reinvigorate your life,
for an honest and hardworking couple as you, I never did encounter.
You deserve to retire as you wished to, to your native Lydia.

Cyno: My darling Kasra there isn't a son more generous
or nobler than you ever.
May the gods protect you forever
and grant you a rule most glorious.

**She hugs and kisses her darling child knowing it to be a final parting
with eyes welled, her tears she could not control from rolling.**

Mitradates: Yes my boy, you have a most benevolent nature
such kindness to us you show.
May the gods protect you and grant you a long and illustrious life.

Cyrus: Thank you father, mother dear
it is the least gratitude a child could upon his parents bestow.
Goodbye, may the gods protect and grant you a most contented life.

**Thus he kissed and hugged his parents and Atash he astride,
and looking back once more Cyrus lovingly did smile
just holding back tears as he saw his mother cry.**

On his return Cyrus had to serve a year more in the *boys* training
before to the ranks of *young men* he was promoted.
At first his peers were a little cool towards Cyrus
believing him to have received a lackadaisical schooling.
A Median grandiloquent returned they him expected
but soon realized the opulent life of Ecbatan had not changed Cyrus.

He was as comfortable with the temperate life of the Persians,
as he had become accustomed to the grandiose of the Medians.
Content once again to eat bread with cress as relish with delectation
and to enjoy a drink of water with equal satisfaction.
Like before, trained he vigorously and proved he was no dandy
and became the first amongst his peers in riding, javelin and archery.

Reverential and obedient of his elders and superiors he remained.
As before magnanimous in defeat and modest in victories he gained.
And once more, high esteem of his peers and superiors he regained.

Act Two
554 – 549 BC Cyrus Takes Media
Part I   Harpagus' Revenge

By the time Cyrus reached manhood, his pre-eminence
for valiance and generosity
and unswerving loyalty
had reached great prominence.
He led several expeditions amongst barbarian marauders
who oft pillaged villagers
on the outskirts of the Persian frontiers.

His fame reached throughout Media
and on his father's death he assumed the throne of Persia.

Meanwhile Harpagus had been biding his time to avenge
the killing of his son and had long desired for revenge.
And in Cyrus he thought he had at last found
the perfect ally to finally realize his design.
Astyages had become increasingly reclusive and unsound,
harsh in temperament, he thought himself divine.

Suspicious had he become of all and none
and enjoyed spreading terror and meting out punishment for fun.
His judgments became completely capricious in nature
to such a point that people stopped their litigation
for fear of imprisonment and execution.
His own relatives lived in fear of incurring his disfavour.

So, it was that Harpagus had garnered support
amongst some of the Median nobles for insurrection.
However all feared and distrusted the other
and as such lacked a leader,
someone they all could trust without fear of betrayal and retribution.
Cyrus, was the perfect candidate who all would willingly support,

Cyrus though a Persian was half Median through his mother.
Well respected was he amongst the Mede nobility
and populace from his time in Media.
So finally Harpagus made his move and sent message to Cyrus of Persia -
A note hidden in the belly of a hare handed he
to his trusted servant Peyam travelling incognito as a hunter.

(In the court of Cyrus Harpagus' servant is welcomed)
Peyam: Sire, I have been instructed by my Lord Harpagus,
to present you with this hare wherein lies his communication,
meant alone for the eyes of the noble King Cyrus.
I am commanded to wait for your response and direction.

**So Cyrus with his dagger cuts open the hare and contained inside
the following message upon a sheep's pelt was so inscribed:**

The time is nigh O son of Cambyses
to rightfully avenge the murderous intent of Astyages.
I am certain you must be aware of how he tried your life to terminate
when you were born, but the gods smiled upon your fate,
for Astyages assigned this heinous task to me.
I though a most loyal of Astyages' men could not such an act carry
I could not an innocent babe slay
and as you may be aware, a high price I did pay
for my disobedience.
Astyages' wickedness and fickle nature was without precedence!

Should you heed my plan you shall inherit Astyages' dominions.
March towards Media with your men and you shall prevail!
The Median troops and generals resistance I promise shall fail
The Medes know you well and hold you in the greatest of affections.
Follow will they you and look upon you as their saviour.
Waste no time and revolt, rid Media and Persia of this evil ruler!

**Having read the message Cyrus pondered the sagacity
of open revolt against his grandfather still so mighty.**

*Tis true grandfather's rule is forever more severe,
with all living in permanent fear.
Though brave and fearless warriors I possess
in numbers we are far less.
And would easily be vanquished should we launch an assault,
for Media has a powerful well ordered force,
But you have Harpagus' word you will face little fight,
and he is a man of his word and not a duplicitous type.
True but still more troops I should gather.
Just in case some resistance we encounter.
So after deep rumination,
he came to the conclusion that the time was ripe for rebellion.*

Cyrus: Peyam, inform your master
soon events will to his satisfaction transpire.

Part II
The Feast

Cyrus bade Harpagus' servant farewell.
And after some cogitation conceived a plan well
on how best to gather to arms his Persians.
Leaders of the principle Persian tribes did he invite
to a grand feast under strengthening friendships' guise:
The Maraphians, the Maspians and the noble Pasargadae
And the tribe from which all Perseid kings sprang the Achaemenidae.
The Germanians engaged in husbandry, the Panthialaeans,
the Derusiaeans, and the nomadic Sagartians,
the Daans, Mardians, and Dropicans,

And what a great banquet it was too,
with the choicest of meats,
bread, wine and many delicious sweets.
With much entertainment too:
Music and singing
Magic and dancing.

Once his guests' had sated their hunger,
Cyrus the following words did utter.

Cyrus: My dear brothers I hope the food and drink was to your taste
and your thirst and hunger it did adequately sate.
Thank you for gracing my humble abode.
Your esteemed presence has much delight me brought.

Adish: *(A portly tribal leader)*
How could we refuse such wonderful hospitality.
It has been a good while since I entertained such gluttony
I only wish you laid more of these gastronomic feasts.
I have a good mind to kidnap your chefs to cook me these meats.
(He heartily laughs)

Cyrus: My dear cousin, if you agree to my proposition
you shall, many such banquets experience on a regular basis
but as for my chefs, were you to deprive me of their service
I would myself strike you a mortal blow without hesitation.
(Everybody bursts out laughter)

Now let me unravel the reason I have requested your presence.
As you know, life has become increasingly toilsome
with the high and exacting taxation
imposed on us by that tyrant Astyages' insistence.

Once a proud and independent nation
but look at us now enslaved to others volition.
Too long have we accepted the lot of subservience!
I would rather die a free man than be in servile obedience!
Tell me are we any inferior in skill or bravery to the Medians.
Of course not! We are their equals! We are a nation of valiant Persians!
So tell me brothers do you desire to remain impotent
or do you wish to rid yourself the yoke of enslavement
and taste once more sweet freedom?

ALL: FREEDOM!!!

Cyrus: Then join me in arms and I promise you manumission.
United we shall overcome the shackles of Mede vassalage!
For Ahura Mazda shall free us from serfage.
And we shall once more soar high on the wings of Providence to liberation.
So rise, for destiny has decreed it so! To Arms! To Freedom!

All: To Arms! To Freedom!

Part III
The Battle For Media

Thus it was that Cyrus united all the Persian tribes in insurrection.
The Persians having grown wearisome of Median rule
had been waiting for a leader such as Cyrus to rebellion.
Aroused by his speech into a frenzy were ready to follow suit.

Learning of the revolt Astyages summoned Cyrus to his displeasure,
and Cyrus did so reply:

Cyrus: Tell Astyages I shall appear sooner for his pleasure
(extreme sarcasm)

Astyages, on receiving such a reply in a fit of fury did fly:

Astyages: How dare that impudent pup me threaten,
with his rabble of an army who I shall bludgeon,
to complete annihilation!

Guards! Summon Harpagus to my court!

Harpagus: How may I be of service my lord?

Astyages: Well Harpagus, you have one more chance to yourself redeem
in my esteem.
I want you to take charge of my army and completely obliterate
Cyrus and his Persian peasants - show no mercy, and them decimate!

Harpagus: You are most kind sire, I hear and obey.
You murderous reprobate!
(He smiles wryly)

This was the moment that Harpagus had long desired
ever since his son like an animal was slaughtered.
Now you shall pay the price of your evil trait

And so it was that Cyrus' army, the Medians in battle engaged
heavily outnumbered but as prearranged
they fought, the few Medes not party to the collusion,
whilst the rest openly fled or to Cyrus made their submission.

On hearing of the shameful desertion
Astyages was consumed by utter rage.
The Chief Magi did he himself with his spear impale.
Then did he experience total humiliation!
As he led the rest of his army outside Ecbatan to defeat,
for some of his men to the other side fled in great speed
while the rest after a valiant struggle finally surrendered.
And the great king himself was captured,
abandoned and in a circle surrounded,
by Harpagus was so taunted

Harpagus: So, my beloved murderous KING
how does it feel to be helpless in a ring?

Astyages: My most trusted Traitor! So, it was you!
I should have had you brought to slaughter
when you first betrayed your most trusting master!
That will teach me to be so forgiving to an ingrate such as you!

Harpagus: Betray, me you!
You heartless demon
you who wished to have your grandchild dead
and when you discovered I had not carried out your evil assignment
then had you slaughtered like a beast my only son as punishment
and unsuspectingly to me fed!
How dare you talk about betrayal and treason!
Gubaru, remove this wretch from my view!
Otherwise I shall surely cut him to pieces myself.
Present him to Lord Cyrus to do with, as he desires himself.

(Astyages before Cyrus in his camp)
Cyrus: So, here we are grandfather – what am I to do with you?
Justice requires you executed for all the people you have wronged
and there is a long list of those who deserve to see you hanged
but I cannot forget your kindness and my kinship to you.

Astyages: Cyrus I ruled like a true king,
to protect such a vast dominion and its treasure
people need not only respect their king
but also fear incurring his displeasure!
Otherwise you will have peasants and vassals in open rebellion
requesting rights above their station.

Cyrus: A king should rule for the good of his peoples
and should not turn them into servile creatures.
A true king through benevolence, compassion and empathy
gains his citizens unconditional love, respect and loyalty.
That grandfather is the true meaning of strength in its truest essence;
for fealty out of fear as you have today found is without substance.

**So it was that after 35 years Astyages lost his precious kingdom
and banished was he from his beloved Ecbatan
and Cyrus the Persian King of Anshan
inherited a vast dominion
stretching to the west beyond the Halys River
and as far east as Bactria.**

Act Three
Part I
King Croesus of Lydia

King Croesus was famed for his wealth and prosperity
his name was synonymous for one extremely wealthy.
To the brim were filled the coffers of his treasury
with precious objects and gold
from his mines and the River Pactolus' sands so old.
An extremely astute and wise soul
He had the foresight to mint coins of silver and gold as currency
to better facilitate the process of commercial exchange.
King Croesus considered himself a man most content and happy.
A great empire had he to his name
that extended to Greek Ionia and Aeolia,
whilst he received tribute from the kings of Asiatic Doria.

One day an agent from Ecbatan to Croesus' court in Sardis arrived
bearing ill tidings of the end of Astyages' rule
Croesus, to Astyages through his sister Aryenis was tied
and through pact of friendship he felt against Cyrus obliged to move.

Agent: I bring terrible news sire!
King Astyages been deposed by his grandson Cyrus of Persia.
This is a perfect opportunity for you to extend your empire
and create a buffer zone in the event Cyrus extends his ambition
towards Lydia's direction,
covetous of the riches of your kingdom.

Croesus: Cyrus! It does not surprise me at all.
Astyages was harsh, coarse and wicked to the core.
I counselled him many a time to curb his intemperate disposition
and be a little forgiving and at least feign compassion
towards his citizens and vassals but ignored he my advice, that old boar.
And now has paid the ultimate price by losing all with his fall.
I shall consult the oracles and see if the gods will smile upon Croesus
were he to pursue military action against Cyrus.

Croesus resolved to despatch messengers
to the different oracles:
Of the Greeks were Delphi, Abae in Phocis, Dodona, Amphiaraus,
Branchidae in Milesia and Trophonius
and Ammon from the Libyan prognosticators,
to trial the veracity of their prophetic powers.
When the messengers returned the scrolls he unfolded
to see what the gods had decided
none but the Delphic oracle in tenor appeared quite auspicious
favouring an attack upon Cyrus deemed it apparently propitious.

It prophesized that should he attack Cyrus the Persian
a great empire he would destroy with his action.
An alliance with the powerful Greek Lacedaemonians it recommended.
The Lacedaemonians happily this call accepted.
For Croesus requesting such a pact had honoured their position
above all the Greeks in military skill and fearless disposition.
They in addition were indebted to him for his past beneficence,
for when they wished to purchase gold of considerable substance
to build Apollo's statue they went to Croesus who of his generosity
gave it free as a gift in charity.

Croesus having misinterpreted the Delphic Oracle thus
decided to make preparations for his foray into Cappadocia,
Media's vassal bordering Lydia.
Just before he was ready to lead his mighty army against Cyrus
Croesus was visited by Sadanis a Lydian Elder
who counselled Croesus thus against such an endeavour:

My Lord you are about to embark upon a course of action
that I plead, will bring you no satisfaction
for should you engage in conflict with Cyrus the Persian
no riches will you gain worthy of mention
his people barely eke out an existence from their rugged nation.
Should you be successful you shall inherit a pitiable dominion
whose coffers will hardly make a worthy contribution.

However, were you to lose, this glorious and blessed kingdom
with its mineral wealth and fecund soil to Cyrus
who once having seen such a wealthy dominion
experiencing its life so pleasant and luxurious
will be want to give it up and consign us to an abject fate.
I beg thee O mighty and sagacious King Croesus,
do not continue with this foolish escapade
as all I see is destruction wrought upon our beautiful land by Cyrus.

Croesus: Dear Sadanis, I have always held you
and your counsel in the highest esteem,
however even you must surely deem,
the words of the Oracle to be true.

It foretold of a victorious campaign
that will further increase my name and domain

**So it was that Croesus all confident of victory
crossed the Halys River with pomp and ceremony
into the Median vassal kingdom of Cappadocia.
He set camp in the district of Pteria
and began ravaging the fields in crop hither and thither.
He besieged Pteria and brought the city
to its knees enslaving the innocent populace without pity.**

Part II
Cyrus' Preparations Against Croesus

**Cyrus' agents soon informed him of Croesus' victory
which was a direct challenge to his authority**

Cyrus: I see, so Croesus takes advantage of Astyages' overthrow!
(Amuses Cyrus on his throne)
Obviously our most illustrious and noble neighbour
believes Cyrus would not dare to incur in battle his disfavour.
Well Croesus you shall soon feel Cyrus' steel for daring to act so!'

Captain Darioush, summon Prince Harpagus.

Darioush: As you wish Lord Cyrus

Harpagus: Yes, my lord - I presume you wish to discuss
King Croesus' assault into Cappadocia.

Cyrus: You presume correct Harpagus.
The wealthy Emperor of Lydia
appears dissatisfied at his wealth
and wishes to accumulate more land by stealth.
(wry smile)

I hear many an oracle he consulted
who success have him comforted.

Harpagus: King Croesus is a most wise and guileful ruler,
he would not have advanced into our empire
without having weighed the consequences of his action.
He obviously deems you too occupied with your new acquisition
and thinks his army as superior to withstand any onslaught.
He possesses a great army, but ours is more than a match to him riposte!

Cyrus: And what of the oracles and the answers they provided?

Harpagus: Well sire, oracles have oft been misinterpreted ….

Cyrus: My grandfather would disagree.
(smiles Cyrus)

Harpagus: Tis true he would indeed disagree.
(he smiles)

Well my lord I have faith in the valour of our men,
they are a most brave and fearless a company of men.

Cyrus: True Harpagus and I have great faith in the brilliance
of our finest general without peer in military artfulness.
(Looking at Harpagus)

Harpagus: You are most kind sire
I am but a humble officer.

Cyrus: Nonsense, you are my noblest general and warrior
whose friendship makes me all the richer.

Harpagus: Thank you for so thinking
and so highly me esteeming.
(Extremely proud of such an accolade)

Cyrus: Well then, delay we must not Harpagus!
For it is bad form to keep waiting our guest most illustrious
He must be feeling lonely and disappointed
that a royal welcome he was not accorded
upon entering Cappadocia.

Harpagus: Indeed sire.
(Both men burst out in laughter at their joke)

Cyrus: Well Harpagus, lets cause a little strife
for our Great King from within his borders,
what say you to sending the Ionians heralds
inviting them to rebellion with promise of vassalry respite.

Harpagus: A most wise move my lord
it always pays to create a little internal discord.

Cyrus: Well Harpagus, it's time to prepare for our march,
I do believe the journey will take days fourteen,
although we must take provisions for at least twenty.

Harpagus: Indeed sire, for who can predict the harsh
conditions, shortages and dangers that may lie unseen,
procuring supplies for such a numerous force may prove a difficulty.

Cyrus: Well, of my Persians there should be 10, 000 in cavalry
a further 20,000 archers and slingers, and around 30,000 in infantry.

Harpagus: Well of Medians, without leaving the country in danger
of King Nabonidus' Babylonian opportunistic vigour,
you can count on 40,000 in cavalry,
40,000 archers and slingers and 50, 000 in infantry.

Cyrus: A substantial force which needs attending
in terms of food, drink, and clothing
as well as medicines, physicians, cooks and bakers.
We also will need to take military men who are skilled carpenters
and smiths and cobblers.
For on such an arduous journey many a repair is needed,
such men can ply their trade for money and be allocated
to particular companies.
They will be exempt from armed duties.

Inform the superintendents of the engineering corps
to furnish me with a list of men who could construct bridges and roads.
In the vanguard of my force they shall stay
thus be called into action straight-away.
And any merchant who may wish to join on our journey
will be welcome provided he does not sell his commodities
before the troops' provisions are near depletion.
If a merchant does not possess sufficient capitalization
to purchase supplies than let him appear before me
with sureties and he shall be provided for from the treasury.

Inform also the granaries to make ready barley, rice and wheat,
not forgetting meat for providing lasting nourishment,
we need such as is preserved, and make procurement
of sufficient cattle, sheep and goats for a fresh treat.

That should be all concerning our preparations,
unless you believe me to have been neglectful of anything.

Harpagus: No my lord, I can think of nothing
you have been most thorough concerning the provisions.

**Within a week sufficient provisions were gathered
for the campaign and the whole force was assembled
outside the palace in Ecbatan, Cyrus in purple regally dressed,
his men thus addressed:**

My dear friends and allies the time is upon us to meet
Croesus who not content at being the richest emperor
has taken advantage of Astyages fall by invading Cappadocia.
He obviously does not believe us able to muster
a large enough force to challenge his greed.

Croesus shall pay with the loss of his beloved Lydia
for wishing to test the mettle of Persia and Media
he will wish he never did cross the Halys River.

Amassed before me I see each and every a brave warrior,
who will pulverize those fancy Lydians with his valour.

Croesus shall feel the wrath of your steel
and no more shall he reign free!

Battle I chose not,
designs upon Croesus' lot I had nought
but now that to humiliate us he has sought.
Ahura Mazda willing he shall suffer a most resounding defeat!
We shall drive him back and take his beloved Sardis in his retreat
and his kingdom as just recompense for our feat!

To everyone I promise an equal distribution
from this parlous expedition
and those courageous souls who fall shall have their portion
distributed amongst their families without procrastination.

Our journey shall be a tough one in the heat of summer,
but it shall harden our resolve and make us all the more hardier,
as for victory we shall be the more hungrier,
while the Lydians shall have become laxed in their peaceful slumber.
So my children make final your preparation,
for tonight we shall ride to our victorious predestination!

**The troops dismissed to barracks, Cyrus did summon
the generals to the palace for a lunch in common
to discuss the march and its formation**

Cyrus: Right gentlemen this is how I propose we arrange our warriors
Chrysantas you shall lead the van, keep to the fore your commanders
and the heavily armed troops with breastplates.
Each company is to follow in a single line,
thus we shall march in safety with the greatest of hastes.
Thus nobody shall fall behind,
for with the slowest leading in advance
our formation will remain unbroken in stance.

Artabazus, you shall head the Persian targeteers and archers.
Then the differing infantries, Gubaru and his Medians,
followed by Embas with the Armenians,
next shall come, Thambradas at the head of the Sacians
and Datamas with that of the Cadusians.
Each captain at the fore of his men shall lead the way.
The archers on the left will stay
with the targeteers on the right
and the camp-followers beside.

Then Harpagus you will head the Median cavalry
with the captains at front leading their men in a single file,
then you Hystaspas with the Persian cavalry
followed by Tigranes and his Armenians, we shall so move in style.

And gentleman, instil in your soldiers,
the importance of marching silently.
We must keep our senses keen
to avoid dangers of ambuscades unforeseen!
Ensure night-watches are changed frequently
that no, one sentinel sleep fatigue conquers.

75

Now gentleman go and ensure all is in order
inform your commanders and troops of their positions.
Neglect not the smallest of details to chance!
Come back to me later
and report to me of the preparations.
This evening we shall march in mighty splendour
I shall make sacrifice for blessings upon our journey.
Ahura Mazda willing we will stride towards victory.

**All prepared, nothing neglected the commanders ensured
that all provisions were taken on board.
In heightened sense of excitement all fell
at the journey ahead,
for many a tale did the men tell
of Croesus' and his riches beyond compare.
Rumour had, that his palace was worthy of the gods' jealous stare.
Sardis' streets were paved with gold it was told.
For Croesus they alleged could transform base metal into gold.
People claimed he had rediscovered the secrets of the alchemist's art of old,**

**A little fanciful but there was no doubting his extreme affluence.
His palace did have many an object golden
from his bed to his bejewelled throne
which dazzled all present in its effulgence
Like a god garbed in purple silken tunics he lived in luxuriance
and reigned in all his manifest glory and opulence.**

**Thus finally Cyrus,
at night did make his march against Croesus.**

Part III
547 BC - The Battle of Pteria

Cyrus had learnt from his father the importance of maintaining
a highly professional and efficient force ever ready to defend
against enemies it sought to fend.
To ensure this Cyrus' men undertook vigorous daily training
in order that their physical strength was meliorated,
and so well drilled that obeying commands became second nature.
Practised they their weapons to improve their skill and stature.
In mock warfare they competed to remain ready for battles anticipated.

This professionalism he maintained even on campaigns journeyed,
he ensured that like at home the soldiers still practised
their skills and maintained discipline ever punctiliously,
adhering the words of his father most scrupulously:

Cambyses: Now my son, it is of paramountcy
that you maintain your men for warfare ever ready,
For your enemies may strike without forewarning.
Thus must you occupy your men in daily training
to keep their physical strength and skill honed perfectly
especially during peace when there is the greatest threat of complacency.

Cyrus: Yes father, but you know many a man finds loathsome
the rigours of daily training and does so without great enthusiasm!
(He smiles)

Cambyses: Indeed my boy it is human nature for men
to avoid strenuous exercise though it be beneficial to them.
However forced training is never a good thing
as troops may come to resent their commander for the training.
The most efficient way to coax your men into exercising
without them you despising - is quite simple - rivalry!
For competition amongst men appeals to their vainglory,
from humble privates to the generals of great glory
will engage in such training with great zeal out of vanity
and pride to be the best amongst their company.
Moreover you must salve your men's apathy with promotion,
honour and distinction.

Cyrus: And how is one to best gain the respect of one's men?

Cambyses: To gain the true respect of one's men,
is not an easy thing, but if you treat all your men
with great kindness, love and equality
from the great general to the simple private the backbone of any army
without whose bravery great victories and glories could never be.
If you have their respect and loyalty than free you will be
from the threat of internal strife and mutiny.
For your men will not wish to bring disgrace upon your dignity.

Further, you must train amongst your men, and do so harder
for if they see their king engaged in training greater
in the rigours of daily exercising
they will be shamed into more vigorous practising.
Training alongside them regularly will breed familiarity.
You will be regarded as a comrade in arms most worthy,
deserving of their life and loyalty.
Remember well Cyrus a distant and haughty king,
cannot, any love or devotion hope for his men to him, bring.

More.. acquaint yourself to as many of your men as you can,
Just imagine a chef who did not possess the sense of taste
or an architect bad at numbers, it would be utter disgrace!
And imagine a general who could not count on his every man?
Thus if you converse to any a high or low ranking man,
without prejudice or favour than all will feel great pride
in their king's recognition of their importance by his side.
Steadfast they will remain, as try they will for you, all they can.

And remember, to expect from your men, courage and valour
always lead from the front, in the face of battle never cower!
Your bravery shall impress upon your men their duty
and they will think you a gallant soul worthy of their loyalty.

78

Cyrus, his father's words well retained,
hard amongst his men, he trained
by nature a very competitive sort
who always wished to become the best at all
he never shirked any mortal encounter
and by example from the front did he lead.
Renowned amongst his men for many a mortal deed
praised highly was he for his great valour.

On their march Cyrus kept his men for battle ready
the troops would train before luncheon and dinner.
Building up sweat before meals he believed necessary
to healthy eating and maintaining
good physical conditioning.

Cyrus wishing for his troops and officers, friendship to engender
on their journey to Cappadocia,
(for men are more willing for comrades to fight
rather than those who they barely know by sight)
had tents made of equal size for each company
which consisted of a hundred men in amity.

As for his tent, Cyrus ensured it big enough to accommodate
those of his men that he wished every day to invite and praise,
for exceptional performance whether it be for impeccable drilling,
great skill in archery, horsemanship or hurling.
It was a great way of knowing the thoughts of his rank and file
and of keeping their morale high.

By nature Cyrus was not a man given to gluttony
and always in moderation he ate
and when he invited his troops, dishes would be laid
before them the like that Cyrus himself ate
and so his men grew to love him more each day
as they discovered their king's humble state,
for endured he conditions the same and travelled not in luxury.

Finally after fifteen days march, they encamped
opposite the Lydians outside Pteria camped.
And Cyrus surveying Croesus' impressive horde
to Harpagus thus spoke

Cyrus: Well my friend, a mighty sight before us, does wait.
Though we outnumber them, they do possess
a fine cavalry more numerous than ours I do declare.

Harpagus: Indeed sire, the Lydians to a sight appear great!
However, I am sure our forces will them impress.
The fame of our warriors is without compare.

Cyrus: Indeed they are Harpagus!
(And then after a moment's pause)
What a beautiful day so calm and peaceful
soon to be interrupted by blood and gore.
May Mazda be merciful and grant us a swift victory.

Harpagus: Tis true Lord Cyrus -
a day most serene and restful,
more the pity than that it will be interrupted by events so raw.
May the gods be gracious and ward off asperity.
(He speaks softly reflecting upon the event that was to unfold)

**There was a moment of deafening silence as thousands arrayed
facing each other as their colourful banners gently swayed
in the breeze awaiting their bloody fate.**

**Cyrus moved along his lines and then when all were ready,
he with his speech roused their minds, thus heady:**

Cyrus: Men, here we are at destiny's gate,
Croesus and his men stand between our victorious fate.
Though they seem formidable, are no match for our resolve,
In the face of our onslaught they will, like salt in water dissolve.
Remember this day and its glories are yours to claim,
immortalized forever you will remain,
so my fearless warriors hesitate not and let's knock on victory's gate!

Then silence once again for a short moment reigned supreme
suddenly broken as Cyrus a resounding CHARGE!!! did sound
that would have brought the gates of hell to the ground
The earth beneath shook and trembled under the thunderous trample
of thousands of hooves and feet as the two armies raced to battle.
Fiercely thousands engaged and in mortal combat many were slain
and even more vicious wounds, did gain -
with the green of the battlefield turned vermillion
with neither side attaining satisfaction.
They finally battle ceased
being extremely fatigued
as darkness slowly enveloped the field.

Cyrus: A bloody and costly day it has proved Harpagus
and we have no advantage to show, over Croesus.

Harpagus: There is always tomorrow sire,
I am sure to victory you shall our men inspire.

Cyrus: I wonder Harpagus.
(Mulls Cyrus)
Off guard we need to take Croesus.
What say you to not attacking tomorrow?

Harpagus: I do not quite follow…?
(Quizzical look)

Cyrus: Well Harpagus, if tomorrow we do not attack,
Croesus will believe in having broken our back
and will return home disbanding most of his army,
So we can take him unawares, as we shall pursue them in secrecy.

Harpagus: A most cunning conception,
Croesus will misinterpret it as a sign of his victorious prognostication.

Cyrus true to his plan the following morrow, feigned flight,
Croesus having suffered heavy casualties did not seek a fight
So Cyrus he did not pursue, deciding a return instead to Sardis,
intending to gather his allies: the Egyptian Pharaoh Amasis,
the Babylonian King Nabonidus
and the Lacedaemonian King Labynetus
hoping the following spring to battle resume.
Croesus thus disbanded his mercenary forces
and headed home content to wait, never did he assume
that Cyrus would march to Sardis having suffered heavy losses.

Cyrus: Well Harpagus, just as I surmised
Croesus is in no state to a victory force,
content to leave he shall soon disperse most of his force
Then pursue him to his Sardis we shall taking him surprised.

Harpagus: Yes my lord, Croesus will I am sure,
head home and call for reinforcements more
at this moment he is most weak.
Once he has disbanded his mercenary force
we must him battle, or else the next time we meet
he shall surely have, the upper-hand with his allied horde.

82

Part IV
546 BC - The Battle of Sardis

**Croesus having disbanded his army was taken completely unaware,
when at 'The Plain of Thymbra' outside his Sardis, Cyrus he did stare.
In haste his forces he mustered.
Two armies for battle facing each other once again gathered.**

Cyrus: Still a mighty cavalry he has retained.

Harpagus: Most magnificent and disciplined he has it maintained.

Cyrus: We shall have to nullify its impact if the day is ours to be claimed.

Harpagus: Well my lord, many years ago when I was a young officer
I had dealings with Scythian raiders.
Their cavalry was a most destructive force
and always gave us a bloody nose.
I oft noticed how horses were always nervous around camels
and on occasions stampeded in terror.
And so on one campaign I decided to attack their cavalry
with the camels brought for our provisions to carry.
The Scythian horses bolted in hurry.

I think the same strategy might work against the Lydian cavalry.
We have around a 150 camels we brought to our provisions carry.
We can mount the camels with armed riders quickly
and charge their cavalry.

Cyrus: My dear friend a master strategist you are without peer
Make it so, today Croesus shall taste a defeat most bitter
for his foolish endeavour!
He will be thrown off-guard and his cavalry shall flee in fear.
The day belongs to us Harpagus and of that I am sure.
Tis time to end Croesus' reign forever no-more.

**So Cyrus summons all his generals to conference
to talk about the troops' formation**

Cyrus: Well gentleman into square formations shall we be.
Harpagus, you shall take charge of the cavalry on the right flank
and you Hystaspas on the left flank.
Araspas you will be in charge of the infantry behind Hystaspas
and you Gubaru with your infantry behind Harpagus.
and you Carduchus the chariots alongside Hystaspas
While Chrysantas shall lead the chariots alongside Harpagus.
And you Dauchus our camel cavalry shall lead
and force Croesus' cavalry in full charge to retreat.
Seeing the camels' hurtling towards them,
the horses in panic will bolt then.
And you Euphrates shall take charge of the mobile towers
with your archers,
positioned in middle of the infantry on the right wing
and you Arsamas of the towers on the left wing.
And that my friends is how arrayed we shall be.

Soon Cyrus' troops in their formation are ready
Croesus tries Cyrus, from all sides to bound.
But as the Lydians turned in their flanks, to him surround,
gaps appeared in their formation making the wings unsteady.

Cyrus: Archers hail down your arrows deadly upon their flanks.

Croesus' cavalry charged forth only to be met by Dauchus.
His camels threw them in disarray, as predicted Harpagus
and finally the battle charge cries Cyrus.

Cyrus: The time is nigh gentleman come follow me –
To Victorrrrrry! To Gloooorrrrry!

Soon Cyrus the most courageous of warrior kings
and his men were engaged in thick hand-to-hand combat.
With little effort Cyrus' men obliterated Croesus' wings.
Most of Croesus' troops took flight behind Sardis' walls in despair.
Cyrus' cavalry then turned to envelop the abandoned heavy Egyptian infantry
who with their long lances had withstood Cyrus' assault with gallantry.
Cyrus impressed by their valour did not wish their slaughter
so he tried to arrange terms for their surrender.

Cyrus: well gentleman, never have I seen such a body of brave men
who remain steadfast in their courage and refuse to give ground.
with our arrows and javelins from afar we could easily them slay
but that would be an insult to their heroic manner.

Hystaspas: Indeed my lord, for never have I witnessed such valour,
to slaughter such a body of men this way,
though we have them at our mercy bound
would be cruel and unjust and blemish the honour of our brave men.

Harpagus: Yes my lord, I suggest we offer them chance to surrender.

Cyrus: Well Gubaru knowing their speech, you can make the offer.
Tell them, should they surrender their arms, no harm they shall suffer,
allowed they will be, to return to their homeland with honour
as they fought with great distinction and valour.

The Egyptians their arms surrendered.
Cyrus laid siege to Sardis whilst Croesus beleaguered
sent fresh heralds beseeching his allies to come to his succour
knowing that besieged Sardis' resistance would soon falter
The Lacedaemons, though closest were engaged in a conflict bitter
with Argives, so promised help to send soon after,
but to Croesus' misfortune Sardis soon fell
before the Lacedaemons and others could send any help.

Part V
The Siege of Sardis

Cyrus: Well Harpagus, Sardis is a veritable fortress.
It has been two weeks now since we laid Sardis to siege
without having discovered any weakness,
unless we take it soon his allies may come to us besiege.

Harpagus: I am afraid his friends presently we may have to face.
Croesus appears for a while to have sufficient supplies.
Sardis has to be taken soon otherwise we may have to engage,
in battle his allies.

Cyrus: Well Harpagus inform the men that their king shall reward
worth any man's weight in gold,
for the first to scale Sardis' wall.

Cyrus made another attempt to Sardis, assail
but with more casualties it did fail.
So, once more the troops retired after receiving a right bruising.
Cyrus could feel the troops moral slowly ebbing
for his soldiers had now been, for many months on campaign
with impregnable Sardis offering Cyrus no gain, only more pain.

However one day Hyroedes, a Mardian soldier did see,
a Lydian soldier drop his helmet down Sardis' side most steep
one facing Mount Tmolus, descend and it retrieve.

Hyroedes from that side resolved, the citadel to climb,
followed by a number of Persians right behind,
men well used to climbing the rugged mountains of Persia
and opened the gates of Sardis and effectively of Lydia.
And so Mighty King Croesus' reign was cut short,
taken prisoner before Cyrus he was brought.

Cyrus: 'O' Croesus why did you attack
one who injury upon you, neither inflicted nor contemplated.

Croesus: My lord, out of familial and friendship ties, I had to act.
To Astyages aid to come - loyalty and duty dictated.

Cyrus: Astyages? Though my grandfather was a crazed oppressor
not worthy of the loyalty of the people of his nation
you know this better than anyone else as brother of my grandmother!

Croesus: What you say is true, he acted like a mad dictator,
and though not worthy of any faithful devotion,
still I was obliged by familial and friendship concord to honour.

I was further emboldened when I consulted the Oracles,
about the expediency of attacking you.
Assured was I of success by the Immortals …
I was informed – if against the Persian I were to move,
a mighty empire I would obliterate.

Cyrus: A mighty empire indeed you did devastate.
Yours! Well, what am I to do with you Croesus?

Croesus: I am at your mercy my Lord Cyrus
I have lost my kingdom and forever am become destitute.

Cyrus: Well, Croesus it would serve no purpose to you execute
after all you are my grandmother's brother.
You shall be banished with your family to Ecbatan as my counsellor.

Croesus: You are most merciful Lord Cyrus,
a most resolute and faithful soul you will find in Croesus.

**After the fall of Lydia the Ionian and Aeolian Greeks sent ambassadors
to Cyrus in Sardis requesting that they become Persian vassals
under the same conditions
as those offered by the Lydians.
However Cyrus answered them by reciting a fable:**

There once was a piper, who played many a beautiful melody,
to seduce the fish to dance ashore,
but the fish at his efforts amused did feel,
till he dropped his pipe and a net brought,
and many a fish he caught.
They started dancing desperately to him please,
to which the piper smiled and thus spoke:
Cease your dancing now for pity!
For where were you when I did play,
the most beautiful melodies for you earlier today?

87

Thus Cyrus to them replied,
for when asked to revolt against Croesus they shied.
So for war did prepare the Aeolians and Ionians,
only from war escaped the Milesians
who to Cyrus
had allied, against Croesus.

Cyrus soon headed back to Ecbatan.
He appointed Tabalus, Sardis' governor
and a Lydian aide Pactyas, to Croesus' treasure gather
and have sent to Ecbatan.

As soon as Cyrus departed,
Pactyas with the treasury at his disposal revolted,
mercenaries he hired and Sardis surrounded.
On hearing of the insurrection Cyrus, Median Mazares appointed,
to swiftly it subdue,
and Pactyas brought before him, to receive punishment due.

On hearing this news, Pactyas Sardis did flee,
but taken prisoner at Chios, he was no more free.
Pactyas was surrendered by the Elders of Chia,
in return for the district of Atarneus a tract of Mysia.

Mazares soon after died whilst on campaign in Ionia,
So Harpagus was sent as replacement from Media.
Harpagus quickly the Greeks of the coast conquered
without a great loss of life suffered.

However, rather than submit, the people of Phocaea and Teos,
abandoned their cities and set shore for Thrace and Chios.
The other Ionian cities were soon subjugated by Harpagus
except Miletus which had a pact with Cyrus.
Harpagus bolstering his troops with Ionians and Aeolians
proceeded to conquer the Carians, the Caunians,
and the Lycians,
soon followed by Cilicia and Phoenecia
thus he completed the conquest of Asia Minor,
and returned a great hero in 542 BC to Media

Part VI
545 BC - Cyrus' Expansion To The East

Whilst Cyrus was preoccupied in Lydia,
The former Median vassal kingdoms of Parthia,
Sogdania, Bactria and Archosia,
saw this as there perfect opportunity to break free.
Trialling thus Cyrus' authority,
which, as inheritor of the Median Empire he could not let be,
for unchallenged his authority would have diminished forever.
Thus Cyrus these former vassals did quickly reconquer
while his trusted general Harpagus was away conquering Greek Asia.

ACT Four
539 - Cyrus & Babylonia
Part I - Babylon

Of the three powers - Lydia, Babylonia and Media
without doubt the greatest empire was that of Babylonia
and Babylon *'Gate of God'* was an awe inspiring sight without peer.
Founded by Nimrod The Great Hunter
on the plain of Shinar on the Euphrates River.
It owed its magnificence to the warrior King Nebuchadnezzar (II)[3].

---

[3] 604 – 562 BC

The city was in the form of a square 14 miles each side
the brick walls of the city were 25 feet thick and 300 feet high.
And a secondary wall 75 feet high behind the former
whose foundations reached 35 feet under.
With 250 towers each 450 feet high, they soared
as the skies they bordered.
By a moat was it encircled,
with the Euphrates flowing through its middle,
it was nigh on impregnable.
At night the city access was closed shut,
its long bridge with drawbridges was hoisted up.

In addition it had 8 impressive gates
leading into the inner city as well as 100 brass gates.

The streets with 3 square feet stone slabs were paved.
The Great Tower *'Ziggurat'* raised high, the heavens graced.
53 temples served the spiritual needs of the city
and altars for Ishtar the Goddess of Love and War numbering 180,
crowned by the Great Temple of Marduk the Chief God most Mighty.

In Babylon Nebuchadnezzar built an imposing palace to be seen,
the like of which had never before been seen.
His temple contained the statute of Baal in pure gold
and a table, both 50 000 lbs weight in gold
with two fearsome lions also cast in gold,
and two human statutes 18 feet high made of solid gold.

But the crowning glory of his treasures and possessions
were the 'Hanging Gardens' the wonder of the ancient kingdoms.
A feat of engineering unsurpassed ever seen
built by Nebuchadnezzar for his Median Queen.
The Euphrates' waters raised by hydraulic pumps kept it green.
Such was the city Nabonidus inherited when king he did succeed.

Clay tablet of Nabonidus praying to the moon, sun and Venus in the British Museum

Part II
Nabonidus & Balshazzar

In 556 BC Nabonidus the last of the Chaldean kings of Babylonia,
from the young King Labashi-Marduk, usurped power,
claiming the throne by marriage to Nabuchadnezzar's daughter,
Nitrocris, widow of Nergal-sharezer.
A nefarious tyrant he reigned with great terror
with complete disinterest in political affairs.
The religion of the Chief God Marduk he did dishonour
as worship to Moon God Sin he did favour.
Into corvee he forced his citizens in utter poverty and despair

Within three years of coming to power
Co-regent he appointed his eldest son Belshazzar
and in 549 BC he decided to reside in the Arabian oasis city of Tayma

(Nabonidus in his inner chamber
speaking with his son Belshazzar)

Nabonidus: My son, I am tired of life in this city, it suffocates me.
These miserable people and their sad little lives I abhor
surrounded by the cronies at court who me no end bore.
From this monstrous Babylon, a break I need.
And so I leave it in your capable keep,
whilst I retire to Tayma, just to be.

Belshazzar: But father how could you leave the luxury
of this great city and live a life in provinciality?

Nabonidus: Quite easily Belshazzar!
I wish away all this for Sin.

Belshazzar: How could you forsake Almighty Marduk father?
Our protector He always has been.

Nabonidus: Marduk! He is but a young upstart, a nonentity!
I have chosen Ancient Sin, the true Deity.
As such I have to leave these servile creatures so nauseating,
who still revel in his worship to me so sickening.

So left Nabonidus for Tayma.
In the tenth year of Nabonidus' retirement to Tayma,
Belshazzar, a great hedonistic feast held for the nobles of Babylonia.

Belshazzar: O nobles today you shall savour an empyrean of feasts,
experience the most delicious of meats,
the most delectable sweets,
every kind of fruit imaginable from my gardens and far.
and to cater for all your needs sublime beauties from near and afar.

And so the guests their voracious appetites to excess sated
and drank from golden chalices once looted
from the Hebrew Temple of Jerusalem's sacking.
Then a drunken lord noticed on one of the walls some writing
which he could not decipher,
Mene, Tekel, Peres
And so he asked Belshazzar:

Noble: My Lord Belshazzar, what do those words up there mean?
For their like I have come across never.

(looking up in surprise)
Belshazzar: They are a mystery, I have never them before seen.
(Looking at his queen)
Is this one of your surprises my dear?

Queen: I am afraid not my Lord Belshazzar.

Belshazzar: Eunach, call onto me the Chief Soothsayer,
let's see if he can throw any light with his powers of augury.
(They all mockingly laugh)
If nothing else he will provide amusement a plenty
as he oft wrecks his little brain figuring out responses of sagacity.
(He mockingly states - once again they burst out in great laughter)

Half an hour later arrives the Chief Soothsayer
in all his paraphernalia

Chief Soothsayer: Y..y ..ou requested my presence … my Loo..rd Balshazzar.
(Huffing and puffing and out of breath arrived a portly old man)

Belshazzar: Yes indeed soothsayer.
A mystery for you I have to resolve, my Seer!
Would you be so kind as to enlighten this audience and me
to the meaning of those words writ upon the wall… there… do you see?

(Gazing up) **CS:** I doo indeed … Erm mmm

Belshazzar: Yeess, O Wise One we await your interpretation?
(He mocks the Chief Soothsayer sarcastically)

CS: I...'m afraid my lord ... the language appears most foreign.
It is neither ... Akkadian nor Sumerian or Median.
It is unacquainted to me ... I am afraid I cannot offer a translation.
(Speaks the CS extremely embarrassed at his lack of knowledge)

Belshazzar: I see, so my Great Soothsayer appears lost for words to be,
now that is a first humble, to see!
(Everybody laughs in mock)

Queen: My lord I have heard of Daniel a Jew
who apparently is a great diviner.
Maybe he'll prove more able then our Chief Forecaster,
being as they say a Messanger,
of the servile Hebrew.

Belshazzar: So ... it appears I have to consult a foreigner,
as our soothsayers are incapable of carrying out their vocation.

You may leave, soothsayer!

CS: But my lord, this Jew is nothing but a fraud ... a false magician!
(He protests)

Belshazzar: Well in that case, you have no humiliation to fear.
Now leave me, for you could do with practising your art a new.
(The CS bows and leaves humiliated)
Guards! Inform the Captain to fetch this Jew!
(The guards bow and inform the Captain of Belshazzar's desire)

**The revellery and debauchery recommences,
as the guests re-engage in their gluttonous behaviour
surrounded by music and laughter,
with nubile girls and handsome youths serving their lords' desire.
An hour elapses before a noble and divine figure the guard announces.**

Belshazzar: So, you are Daniel the Jew!
It appears you possess the prophetic light of the lucky few.

Daniel: I have been blessed with the gift by The Almighty God,
my lord.

94

Belshazzar: Well than let's see if your ALMIGHTY God
can aid you in interpreting the mystery of the words upon that wall.
(Challenges Belshazzar)

Daniel: Well … my lord, of each word the following is its meaning:

Mene – Your kingdom God has numbered and brought to termination!

Tekel – You have been weighed in the balances and are found wanting!

Peres – Your kingdom is divided and given to the Mede and Persian!

Belshazzar: Well Jew! As you can see I am frightened and quivering.

**Belshazzar feigns halfheartedly, a frightened quiver
as his pulse rises knowing the words to be true in nature**

We are perfectly aware of that Persian runt Cyrus
and have made provisions a long while for his sights covetous.
Do you not know Babylon is an impregnable city?
(He raises his tone)

Daniel: That may be true but it has been decreed so by The Almighty.
Repent my lord, for it is not too late!
(Pleads Daniel)

Belshazzar: Me Repent! Guards! Drag out of my sights this slave!

**However once Daniel leaves, an air of resignation
all the guests are by consumed.
The revellery by Belshazzar is brought to termination,
as all recognize the words of Daniel with truth to be imbued.**

Part III
Cyrus' Preparations For Babylonia

**Meanwhile, Cyrus after having conquered most of Asia
and firmly established his rule as a just and fair emperor
finally turned his attentions to the greatest prize of Babylonia.
Ever since he assumed his throne,
he believed himself moved by a Higher Authority
which had guided him to greatness, never before known,
who with Babylonia Cyrus would crown and him grant supremacy.**

Cyrus: My Dear Harpagus the time has come to fulfill destiny,
Babylonia cries to us in pain and agony.
Nabonidus and his son Belshazzar are despised,
by their people and vassal kingdoms.
Tis time, its people from tyranny were delivered
and enjoined into our fold of nations.

Harpagus: The time is most auspicious my lord.
In Tayma remains still Nabonidus
and Belshazzar is no match for the the warrior king Cyrus.

Cyrus: You are most kind Harpagus,
and you are indeed right Balshazzar is no Nabonidus
and in battle untried, what do you think Croesus?

Croesus: I agree my lord, Belshazzar is not tried in battle,
and shall prove no match for your mettle.
By the time Nabonidus learns of your incursion
he will be too late in battle to make any impression.

Cyrus: Indeed! Well than it's time to head in the westerly direction.

(Two weeks later Harpagus reports to Cyrus on prepartions)

Cyrus: Come in my friend, I believe good news you bring onto me?
All is prepared, I presume?

Harpagus: Indeed sire, you can rightly assume,
and await your command now we.

Cyrus: Then Harpagus, tomorrow we shall for Babylonia ride!
Mazda willing, we shall take it without a great fight.

(Next morn outside the palace in Ecbatan)
Cyrus: Well Harpagus a beautiful September's morning
to bid us well on our journey.

Harpagus: Indeed sire, it would appear from the sun's energy
the gods are smiling.

Cyrus: Of that I am sure, for I feel the hand of The Almighty,
beckoning us onto victory

Part IV
The Fall Of Opis

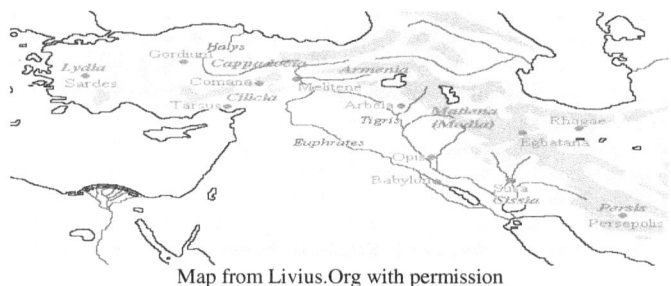

Map from Livius.Org with permission

And so a maginificent procession of might finally departed,
arriving a week later at the ancient city of Opis
situated west of the River Tigris
sitting on the eastern banks of the Diyala so free flowing
from the Matienian Mountains, the waters of the mighty Tigris finally swelling.
On the banks of the River Diyala facing Opis, the mighty force halted.
Cyrus all surveyed and reflected.

Harpagus: It appears the waters are too deep to ford,
and crossing by ferry would be most precarious, my lord.

Cyrus: We could channel its waters though it may take a while.
However, it behoves us to value each man's life.
Tragic it would be to lose any of of them so cheaply,
especially as they have shown me such unswerving loyalty.

And so 180 trenches on each side of the river
the army created,
dispersing the river's water,
And finally towards Opis they headed.
The Babylonians outside the walls of their city waited.
The armies facing each other confronted.
Cyrus to the Median Gubaru command handed,
Gubaru charged and there ensued a short battle.

The Babylonians with little love for Balshazzar,
for defeat settled.
The citizens of Akkad on hearing Opis' fall,
siezing their chance rebelled with great gall,
but like animals they were slaughtered,
by the blood-thirsty Balshazzar.

Cyrus: You have done well Guburu,
that was most swift a victory.

Gubaru: They were no match for our army sire.
The Babylonians for battle had no desire
I but led the men to certain success as they offered no fighting desire.

Cyrus: You are most humble Gubaru,
and sell short your skill and bravery.

Gubaru: My lord is most kind in his estimation of me,
I thank him for his high praise which he deems me worthy.

**And so Cyrus entered the city to great cheer
and addressed the populace, telling them him not to fear.**

Cyrus: O people of Opis, from us you have nothing to fear.
For we come neither to pillage nor plunder your glorious city.
We come instead to deliver you from servitude free.
To the tyrant Nabonidus and his son', bound you are no-longer!

For your loyalty, equality you shall receive in my kingdom,
you shall not be inferior of any Persian.
You can once more live your life in freedom,
practicing your customs and laws as before without apprehension.

**The whole crowd erupted in great cheer
and blessed the coming of Cyrus as their saviour not conqueror.**

Cyrus: I do believe they have warmed to me Harpagus.
(He waves to the jubilant crowd)

Harpagus: They have every reason to do so, Lord Cyrus.
They have been freed from the bonds of tyranny.

Cyrus: Well, we shall sojourn for a while to rest our men most weary
and replenish our provisions full and then on to Sippar for victory.

Part V
Towards Sippar
<u>A</u> – Cyrus & Araspas Debate The Charms of Beauty

The Babylonians of Sippar like of Opis quickly crumbled,
offering little resistance in face of such a mighty army,
Cyrus forbade his troops from looting or pillaging the city
though as victors, to the spoils of war they were entitled.

Instead they claimed their compensation, monetary
from the city's treasury.
Amongst the spoils of battle was the Lady Pantheia,
wife of Abradatas of Susa.
By chance he was on a mission to India for Nabonidus,
to garner support against Cyrus.

One of Cyrus' loyal companion Araspas of Media,
an old friend from the time he spent with his grandfather,
had set aside this Lady for Cyrus, as befitting an emperor.
Cyrus chose not to enter the palace of Sippar
preferring instead to remain outside the city
with his men most happy.

(Araspas enters Cyrus' camp to inform him of the proceedings)
Cyrus: So my friend, how are things moving?

Araspas: Well my lord, the officials are most obliging,
furnishing us with a list of the contents of the treasury.
They appear rather pleased to be rid of their rulers.

Cyrus: A the result of years of oppression and tyranny,
It appears the Babylonian's are not fond of their masters.

Araspas: Indeed they are not, and for you my lord,
I have unearthed a resplendent treasure worthy of a god.

Cyrus: Really? Pray tell me of this treasure most hallowed?

Araspas: Well my lord, when the palace we entered,
we discovered the most graceful sublime vision,
A seraphic beauty worthy of idolization.

Cyrus: An angel worthy of veneration?
(Smiles Cyrus)

Araspas: Yes sire, the Lady Pantheia,
wife of Abradatas of Susa,
apparently on ambassadorial duty to the kingdom of India
to seek alliance against you for Babylonia.
You must judge her beauty yourself sire.

Cyrus: Well my friend, if the lady is such a wondrous beauty,
then it's best that I do not see her.

Araspas: You do not wish to see her?
(Extreme surprise)
After all I have related about her beauty!

Cyrus: My dear Araspas,
if she is as beautiful as you say
then the lady may well cast her spell upon me
making me slave to her will
to the neglect of my duties as a king to my men.

Araspas: How could that possibly be my Lord Cyrus?
Though a heavenly presence, be she may,
surely we are all masters of our destiny.
Only the base, are unable to temper their will,
not the likes of you or I as *real* civilized men!

Cyrus: Dear Araspas many a great man has come to harm
enslaved to female charm.
As mortals, reason at times of weakness temptation destroys.
It is far better, if a man such lures avoids,
then tread its enchanting trail
and fall, to it prey.

Araspas: I would like to think I had control over my temptations,
and was not so base as to give in to my passions.
Otherwise what differentiates us from bestial behaviour,
if we were not able to temper our concupiscent fire?

Cyrus: Indeed my friend.
But though man's soul can reason between right and wrong,
yet trapped it is in flesh, in the physical realm.
As such it is prey to the physical attractions so strong
for just as the moth knows of the dangers of fire
yet it remains helpless in its desire
and perishes in flames for its fiery predilection
and so too, it is hard for the body to curb its base inclination,
though it may lead to its annihilation,
It is inescapably spellbound by its pernicious song till its end.

Araspas: Yes my lord, but I still contend
that it is possible to curb with training, one's passions
or else we would have chaos with people lost to temptations,
not only coveting what others have
but actually acting upon their desires without care,
and taking by force as they might another's right
because they were greater in might.

Cyrus: As I know you, most noble and temperate to be,
in your charge shall I entrust this Lady
until we have in Babylonia, completed our campaign,
for if I see such a beguiling beauty, I might go insane.
(Both smile)

Araspas: Fear not sire, though she is an undoubted wonder
Araspas' shall to her charms not surrender.

Cyrus: Thank you my noble friend.

B - Araspas' Enchantment

Poor Araspas though most loyal a friend,
quickly fell under Lady Pantheia's spell.
Each day she grew to him ever lovelier
by the grace and nobility of her character.
Mesmerised was he by her soft melodic hex
for each time she spoke he felt caught in a reverie,
till finally one day when he no-more felt free
as his heart the ache of love could no-longer contend.

Thus we find Araspas in Pantheia's camp plead

Araspas: Dear Lady Pantheia,
I can suppress my love for you no-longer
I only exist when you are near,
and when parted your presence I crave and hunger.

Pantheia: My dear Araspas, please speak of love no-more.
Though you are a most kind and gentle soul
I could love you never,
for my heart to my husband, is tied for ever.

Araspas: I am hopelessly in love with you Pantheia!
Without you I am made destitute,
since the day I gazed upon sublime you
I only live for the thought of you.
In time I know, I can make you love me true,
so I beg you, please be mine Pantheia!
(He pleads)

Pantheia: My dear Araspas,
please forgive this lady if her superficial beauty led you astray
but her love is eternally bound to her Lord Abradatas
So I beg of you please, about love no-more articulate

Rejected and dejected Araspas leaves
but the fires of passion ablaze did remain
and tormented he vowed to her gain.
Driven by loves madness he no longer sleeps.

Meanwhile

<u>C</u> - Lord Gobyras' Story

The following morning in rode Gobyras
an elderly Assyrian nobleman on his sleek snow-white steed,
accompanied by a cavalry of a thousand of the finest sorts.
An upright and confident man with shoulder-length silver locks
that gently cascaded in the kindly breeze,
and with an immaculately kept beard, he came seeking Cyrus.
Outside Cyrus' camp he was met by Chrysantas,
a most trusted Persian captain of Cyrus.

Gobyras: I wish to speak to your King Cyrus.

Chrysantas: And who may I say seeks our Lord Cyrus?

Gobyras: An Assyrian nobleman, Gobyras.
I wish to make my domain and troops at your king's disposal.

Chrysantas: Well you may enter Lord Gobyras,
but your cavalry to move any further are granted refusal.

Gobyras: Then let it be!
Men wait here for me!
*(Gobyras accompanies Chrysantas to Cyrus's tent and waits while he is
announced)*

Cyrus: Enter my Lord Gobyras,
you must be tired after your journey,
may I offer you something refreshing.

Gobyras: Greetings Lord Cyrus.
My travel was neither long nor involved great difficulty
but a cup of water, to my lips would be most pleasing.

Cyrus: Ah heavenly water,
after a journey, no sweeter, a nectar.
(One of Cyrus' attendants pours for Gobyras a chalice of water)

Cyrus: So Lord Gobyras, you wish to avail your services to us?
Pray, why thus?

Gobyras: Well Lord Cyrus, let it be known I am no traitor
and was a most loyal servant of my Lord Nabonidus.

However, since he abandoned Babylonia to his son Balshazzar
I can no-longer, him my loyalty offer.
For Prince Balshazzar is responsible for turning
this once happy soul into a worthless human being

Cyrus: What did he do to erase
your happy state?

Gobyras: Well my lord, last summer my life ended.
My one and only beloved son, Prince Balshazzar did kill.
The Prince open hunt did hold,
with no deference to their lord
a trial of skill to see the first to shoot a gazelle still.
The prince's arrogance victory dictated.

Balshazzar was the first to eye a gazelle and gave chase
followed quickly by my boy in great haste.
The prince shot the first arrow
but missed by a hairs' length narrow.
Woe be to the gods for not making his aim truer,
for a father would still have his son near!
The gazelle on air sped
as my boy aimed it dead.

All the nobles congratulated my boy except the prince
who embarrassed and enraged by his poor aim did wince.
Barely containing his anger he plotted his revenge.
The hunt continued for some hours longer
when the company came upon an alpha lion to fear
the prince feigning aim for the wild beast
struck my son with his evil deed.

And that miserable day
my life faded away!

Cyrus: I wish there were words which I could utter
to take away pain so severe;
unfortunately words such a loss, could compensate never.

105

Gobyras: Well my lord, I wish to see my brave son avenged
as such all that is mine to command I present to you;
A thousand strong cavalry,
and ten thousand strong infantry.
And under my governance a wide domain to pay you tribute
should you help my son revenged!

Further, I have my most beloved and beautiful daughter
who I would be happy in marriage to you offer.

Cyrus: Thank you Lord Gobyras for your most grateful offer.
I hereby promise to you and Ahura Mazda
that Balshazzar for his crime shall be made to answer.
But tell me Lord Gobyras how is one to trust a stranger?

Gobyras: Well my lord, I shall bring forth all my treasure,
and lay it at your alter
and above all my only daughter
I shall to you offer
as a sign of my avowed loyalty
and constancy.

Cyrus: That won't be necessary;
you appear a lord of your word most honourable and worthy.
Tell me, are there others like you injured by Balshazzar's whimsical nature
who may consider rebellion against this capricious creature?

Gobyras: Well there is one other nobleman
who has suffered even more than I
Gadatas is his name, most honourable and handsome
and far more powerful and richer than I.
The city of Der is his dominion.
Once, fickle Balshazzar's close companion;
his beauty was his only transgression.

It happened one day
that Balshazzar's concubine of the day
commented on Gadatas' beauty and grace:
how any lady would be most fortunate to be his concubine
let alone his chosen bride find.
Consumed with jealousy and rage,
he had Gadatas eunuch made.

The Prince justified his heinous crime,
claiming Gadatas had designs upon his concubine.
Poor Gadatas to live with the knowledge each day
that he will never be able to father a child
to carry his name must burn him from inside
and helpless like me to avenge his unfortunate fate.

Cyrus: Poor man to have his manhood taken away
at the cruel whim, of a heartless ruler's jealous craze
must surely be beyond any pain, conceivable.
Do you think he would, to rebellion be amenable?

Gobyras: I am sure he would, to that suggestion be most agreeable;
finally a chance to avenge his burning rage.

Cyrus: Could you on my behalf inquire of his rebellious state?

Gobyras: Well Lord Cyrus I will for you inquire
but must now beg of you leave.
You would do me great honour to guest at my keep.
It is but three days ride, and I promise you and your warriors
shall receive a welcome most warm and salubrious.
I will leave one of my men, to you guide clear.

Cyrus: Thank you Lord Gobyras we shall pass by your place
seeking from war for a few days grace, in a friendly place.

**Cyrus bade Gobyras good journey.
Two days later Cyrus and his army
for Gobyras' castle made start
with the infantry in the vanguard
followed by the cavalry in the rear.
By the third evening as they approached near,
from a distance an imposing fortification arose,
a mighty castle perched on air upon a steep slope.**

**Cyrus and his men were impressed by such a sight,
when they came upon the castle they were in awe,
strong and resolute against enemies it stood unyielding.
Cyrus around it rode, a weak spot seeking
but none he saw;
it was far too firm to yield easily without a heroic fight.**

Provisions enough to last a year they probably did store
protection against being besieged like most forts in Babylonia,
who food enough had hoarded for a few years... maybe more.
Having seen Cyrus take Media and Lydia
Nabonidus realised, Cyrus would not wait long before
he turned his attentions to Babylonia.

Gobyras bade Cyrus enter some of his men inside
and report back to him of what lay inside.
He himself had only recently returned, from having Gadatas visited.
Good news had he, for Gadatas, Cyrus' proposition had heartily accepted.

Cyrus: Well, Chrysantas you are a most astute soul
so pick a few men to wander inside and report.

Chrysantas: Yes my lord.

On his return after a few hours Chrysantas so reported

Chrysantas: Well sire, as you rightly imagined
they have provisions enough for a few years gathered.
With, huge granaries, thousands of cattle, sheep and poultry,
many a fruit tree and vegetables growing abundantly
many wells we saw, thus of water they do not appear lacked.
As for arms they look well prepared,
thousands of arms of all kind did we see in store
and a great supply of iron to forge many more.
All in all it would be extremely difficult to besiege or assail.
Gobyras' castle would come at a price very high to pay.

Cyrus*: Is that so ... (thinking to himself) it would appear
Gobyras wishes to show us his strength and vigour.*

And as Cyrus cogitated Gobyras came out with some of his men
carrying wine, flour, bread, cattle, goats, sheep,
and condiments – provisions aplenty for a great feast
for Cyrus and his tired and hungry men.
Everything was apportioned equitably
and the cooks and bakers set about the preparations busily.

Cyrus: you are a most generous host, Lord Gobyras
I am humbled by your offerings in abundance, so.

Gobyras: You are most welcome Lord Cyrus,
the least I could do and hopefully I maybe of service more.
I would be most honoured if you banqueted with me in my hall
tonight Lord Cyrus?

Cyrus: Thank you for the invitation,
but you have been more than cordial
and it is time that we were to you a little convivial,
thus extend to you I, our banquet invitation.

Gobyras: You are most kind my Lord
and I would be happy so to accept your invitation.

Cyrus: As for your daughter have no fear,
for in my company I have many an upright and noble man
who would be worthy of her hand
although in monetary terms, they compared to you are much poorer.

Gobyras: By Marduk! Lord Cyrus please show me these individuals
so honourable and noble,
(He smiles)
for I would rather give my daughter's hand to these virtuous souls
than ones of wealth and riches but ignoble.

Cyrus: Point them I will not Gobyras but dine with us tonight
and gaze upon many a worthy sight.

So Gobyras in the evening for dinner regally dressed arrived
but was struck by the simplicity of the food and décor.
Cyrus the great emperor and his men sat him before,
on straw mats with a few couches for comfort but no more.
He thought his people more refined and civilized.
But he soon changed his estimation,
when he observed Cyrus and his generals eating.
All sat calmly and ate their food with great moderation,
though it was obvious they were after a long journey starving,
but at the sight of meat did not give to voracious consumption.

Gobyras was struck by the way Cyrus and his men,
each himself served an equitable portion,
the first ones did not take advantage of their position,
by helping themselves to more than the last person.
Such camaraderie never did he observe amongst the men,

They ate and conversed with great drollery,
that Gobyras finally understands,
how Cyrus came to conquer so many lands.
These men were not some rude soldiers
but educated and refined scholars.
With respect and deference to Gobyras they spoke.
Each he presumed to be a most powerful lord,
yet their tongue was neither harsh nor coarse
but soft and mellifluous to the ear it was,
animated with great verve and raillery.

Cyrus: Tell me Gobyras do any of my companions appear
worthy for your daughter, a suitor?

Gobyras: I am afraid that would be a very difficult decision
for had I come across any one of them,
I would deem him a most worthy man
for my daughter's hand,
for never have I come across so many gentle natured men,
who for their peers have such a genuine love and affection.

Many a nobleman have I seen, Lord Cyrus
over the years in the court of Nabonidus
but none a finer company was presented as today before Gobyras.

Cyrus: So Lord Gobyras, what of your riches so fine,
how do you think they compare to mine?

Gobyras: My lord you are far richer than I could ever be
even if I possessed all the gold in this world, it would never to yours compare,
for you possess treasures beyond my wildest expectations
the great love and affection of such companions.
Loyalty and amity that's beyond superficial wealth to compare,
which is why Lord Cyrus, I could never so rich as you ever be.

Cyrus: Indeed Gobyras rich is the man
who has the love and loyalty of such comrades to hand
I would never trade such friendship, for all the treasuries
of this temporal world and its perfunctory courtesies.

Gobyras: In your companions you possess
a most wondrous treasure to bless.

Cyrus: You are most kind Lord Gobyras.
(As with such high praise he is embarrassed)
Pray tell what news of Lord Gadatas?

Gobyras: Well Lord Cyrus I had occasion
to meet him on my way from whence I left you,
and I myself only arrived a few hours before you.
Gadatas has agreed at Sippar to join you
as happy is he to ally to your kingdom.

Cyrus: Thank you Lord Gobyras,
that is reassuring to know,
for I would much rather friend him behold,
than to have him enemy along with Balshazzar and Nabonidus.

111

Part VI
Sippar's Fall & The Babylonian Lord Gadatas

So after three days repose,
once more the great army up and rose.
And on October 9 under the cover of night
to Sippar they arrived.

Cyrus: Well gentleman, there before us is the famed Sippar.
Only it stands between Babylon our cherished prize.
Tonight we shall make camp and tomorrow at sunrise,
see if it is open to persuasion, or combat its chosen desire.

So the army camped and in the morning,
they were suddenly awoken by thunderous hooves galloping,
all thought the Babylonians to have so early made their opening,
However, it was only the resplendent Gadatas with his army
a 1000 strong in cavalry and 10,000 in infantry.
Astride on his fiery ebony steed,
He posed an imposing sight of strength and beauty.
All in awe of his presence they seemed.

Gadatas: I am Lord Gadatas,
I seek your King Cyrus.

Captain: I am Captain Darioush
Come this way Lord Gadatas.

**So Darioush takes Gadatas,
to see Cyrus**

Darioush: My Lord, the Lord Gadatas, awaits your pleasure.

Cyrus: Well lets not make our friend wait, or he may believe us rude in character.

(Gadatas Cyrus' tent enters and Cyrus extends a warm welcome)

Cyrus: Greetings My Lord Gadatas.

Gadatas: Greetings My Lord Cyrus.

Cyrus: Lord Gobyras' high esteem, of such presence and noblity,
was placed befittingtly.

Gadatas: Thank you Lord Cyrus
Lord Gobyras is most kind in his praise.

Cyrus: Come sit here Lord Gadatas
join us[4] and your repast break.

Gadatas: It would be an honour Lord Cyrus.

(They sit and discuss the hurdle of Sippar before them)

Cyrus: So, what counsel can our Babylonian Lords afford us?

Gadatas: Well my lord,
it would be expedient to negotiate with Sippar's commander.
I know him of old.
When he learns of our renunciation of Balshazzar,
and the overwhelming force arraigned before his stronghold
he will be more than eager to surrender.

Cyrus: Then, Lord Gadatas,
I entrust to you the task of negotating the surrender.

Gadatas: As you wish Lord Cyrus,
I am sure we can avoid great slaughter.

**The Babylonian general having seen the might
before arrayed took fright,
and agreed to the surrender
for he also had no great love for his emperor.
So opened he Sippar's gates and Cyrus did enter,
and address the public who gave him a rapturous cheer.**

---

[4] Harpagus, Gubaru, Hystaspas, Chrysantas, Araspas, Gobyras, Artabazus

Cyrus: O citizens of Sippar I have come neither
to enslave nor to loot or pillage your city.
I come not as tyrant but liberator!
Your laws, and way of life I guarantee,
forsake me not and I shall remain your faithful protector!

And like in Opis the citizens of Sippar enthusiastically,
Cyrus did receive,
glad to be once again free
from the rule of tyranny,
For Nabonidus and Belshazzar did rule most cruely.

Cyrus: It would appear the people of Sippar
no great love for their beloved emperors harbour.
(Smiles Cyrus with great satisfaction)

Harpagus: Nabonidus and his son ruled most harshly
with no respect for religon or tradition
and treated their citizens with condescenion
forced to labour for their beloved emperors for free.

Cyrus: Well Harpagus, so finally to glorious Babylon
and it won't be so easy.
We can expect fierce battle at this fabled bastion.
We will have to use all our cunning and bravery,
to wrestle it free from Balshazzar's captivation.

Harpagus: True sire, but with you to lead and inspire
we cannot but defeat Balshazzar's fire
For the men you love, like a father
and would willingly follow you to hellfire.
Belshazzar could such loyalty never, with money hire.
His fealty is borne out of intimidation and fear.

Cyrus: Indeed Harpagus, true loyalty is borne out of love and respect,
not of arrogance and contempt of one's fellow man.
Providence willing, the tyrants' swift defeat we shall plan.
Well, my friend a few days ride more to Babylon, so let's lead our van,
and Providence's grand design put to effect.

Meanwhile

<u>A</u> - Araspas' Pain

**Poor Araspas though he tried his foremost,
had fallen madly in love with Pantheia
and once again approached her,
determined to make her his, whatever the cost!**

Araspas: O Pantheia, I'm driven to distraction by you
ever since I gazed upon your sublime beauty....
sleep, reason and appetite have deserted me.
I wander aimlessly like a man driven by love to insanity ....
Wherever I look, your heavenly image before me, I see.
Your dulcet voice in my head pursues me constantly
I love you with passion Pantheia! I beseech you, mine be!
I will be your slave for all eternity.
O Pantheia I can no-longer live without you!

Pantheia: My dear Araspas, I am not worthy of such worship.
I have no wish to make you a slave.
You are a noble and virtuous soul, most brave.
You shall find a woman more deserving of such affection.
However my dear Araspas, I am not worthy of such adoration,
for my love is meant for no other than my beloved Abradatas.
So I plead to you dear Araspas,
please forget me, for I am undeserving of such worship.

Araspas: It is too late Pantheia,
I am yours! I need you and by Ahura Mazda
I shall if needs be by force become your lover and master!

**And so poor Araspas once more faced with frustration
resolves the next time to press his will harder.
Pantheia fearful of Araspas' amorous desire
sends word to Cyrus, seeking his protection.**

**On receiving Pantheia's plea,
Cyrus smiles fondly,
remembering his friend's naivety,
concerning the enchantments of beauty,
like many before, he was by it charmed into captivity.**

Cyrus: Well Artabazus, it would appear
our friend like many a man prior
has fallen prey to the charms of female splendour.

Artabazus: Indeed he has sire,
having seen the Lady Pantheia myself,
I am surprised it has taken this long
for Araspas to act upon his amorous desire.
His mind appears, from here gone.
He has kept himself to himself.

I've even heard him rebuke, one of his captains mistakenly,
for a command that he gave wrongly.
(Both men smile)

Cyrus: Ah … the wonders of love.
It is a good thing I did not gaze upon Lady Pantheia;
for, like Araspas I would have been driven mad with desire.
I think it would be best if you alleviate him of her temptation
for I fear he will act upon his passion,
and later will feel embarrassed of his enslavement to love.

Artabazus: As you wish sire,
I shall relieve poor Araspas of love's burning fire.

**Now Artabazus, being quite a humorous soul,
could not resist such an opportunity for a joke,
so with Araspas he feigned Cyrus' displeasure
and rebuked him harshly for his behaviour.**

Artabazus: Do you know why I have come, Araspas?

Araspas: Enlighten me Artabazus.

Artabazus: Well my most virtuous friend…
it has come to Lord Cyrus' understanding
that you, a mere officer,
dared make amorous designs upon Lady Pantheia,
the Lady, Cyrus entrusted to you as his loyal companion.
I must say Araspas you've brought shame upon your person
by daring to take the belonging
of one who treats you with such amity and favour, O ungrateful friend!

Thus, cruel Artabazus brought Cyrus' *'rebuke'* to an end,
barely containing his laughter, at the shame felt by his friend.

Araspas thus feeling greatly ashamed,
slumps his head, guilty and disgraced,

Araspas: I could not help it Artabazus
that Lady, my soul has captivated
and I am ashamed to say
I would have been her slave,
for eternity had she me accepted.
What a lowly wretch I have behaved Artabazus.

Artabazus: Well it is a good thing Lord Cyrus
has discovered your shameful behaviour.
You are to accompany me Araspas!
Lord Cyrus wishes to speak to you, about your disloyal nature.

Poor Araspas little realising the joke played,
followed Artabazus dejected and ashamed
awaiting his ignominious fall from Cyrus' favour.
How would he face him with honour?
His friend and king he did lecture
about conquering one's base passionate nature.

(Araspas enters Cyrus' tent.
Artabazus stays outside and listens with intent)
Cyrus: Come in my dear friend, and what brings you here?

Araspas: You sire,
Artabazus said you wished to see me
about my disgraceful behaviour
concerning Lady Pantheia.

I am ashamed of my conduct so reprehensible, sire
I am ready for whatever punishment that you deem me worthy.
I was so arrogant as to suppose that I could suppress my desire
for that most virtuous of ladies, Pantheia.

A reprobate have I become, sire
of your friendship unworthy.
A traitor unable to temper his amorous desire!
Wronged have I you my Lord, and the goodly Lady Pantheia.

Cyrus: Traitor? Punishment?
My dear friend whoever spoke of punishment.

I simply informed Artabazus to relieve you of such a burden.
Traitor! Araspas my dear friend and confidant – Never!
The fault was mine leaving you open to beauty's enchantment,
you remain blame free, for many a saint has fallen at beauty's alter.
(And he smiles affectionately)
I do believe our friend Artabazus
has been up to his mischievous games Araspas.

**Artabazus, who had been listening outside all the while,
enters the tent with a most innocent smile.**

Artabazus: And how is our virtuous young man, Lord Cyrus?

Cyrus: The culprit up to his usual raillery.
How could you put our friend through such pain, Artabazus?

Artabazus: Quite easy sire, I just could not resist the opportunity.

**They all burst out in great laughter
though Araspas still a little in discomfiture,
ashamed of not his passions being able to temper.**

Araspas: Artabazus, you rascal!
I shall have my revenge, you scoundrel.
And you sire,
are a most forgiving lord and master.

Cyrus: Dear Araspas, your friendship and loyalty
is most important to me,
now let's speak no more of this matter.
Come join us as I do believe it is time for supper
(They all smile)

B - Pantheia & Abradatas

The Lady Pantheia, to show Cyrus her appreciation
requested he allow her to send for her husband
who most grateful for the respect to her given
would gladly join the ranks of such a noble leader
for he too had no love for Balshazzar,
who on many an occasion had shown amorous designs upon her.
Cyrus agreed, being for allies most eager.
Thus Pantheia sent to Abradatas her messenger.
Abradatas on receiving news of his beloved Pantheia,
rode like the wind, yearning so to be beside her.
And after two days arrived in Cyrus' camp a noble young warrior,
of about 30, attired gloriously in burnished armour
his helmet plumed with a scarlet feather,
standing in a glimmering chariot, worthy of his high station,
pulled by four fiery black steeds, scions of devilish impregnation
offering his services at the head of ten thousand men of distinction.

Abradatas: Please inform Lord Cyrus, that Abradatas of Susa,
husband of Lady Pantheia is here.

On being informed of Abradatas' appearance,
Cyrus informed Captain Darioush to lead him to Lady Pantheia
and request he appear before him in the morning for an audience.
Overjoyed, Abradatas once more has in loving embrace his beloved Pantheia.

Abradatas: My darling Pantheia,
distraught have I been ever since I heard of your capture.
Death would taste sweeter
then a life without you so bitter
I ceased to be, when I discovered you taken at Sippar.
The worst I did fear.
To be here before you, in your loving embrace
is the sweetest of Marduk's grace.

Pantheia: My lord, my love …how lonely I've been without you, near.
Thrown was I into utter despair the day I was taken prisoner ….
My happiness ebbed away fearing us parted forever
even though I've been treated most kindly, by the Persian Emperor.
For though, Cyrus won me as his possession
he has not once gazed upon my person
but instead has granted me his protection.

119

Abradatas: This Cyrus appears to be a noble and righteous soul.
I cannot believe my eyes, is it really you beside, my Pantheia.
My sweet intoxication, happiness has returned once more,
and this time I promise to leave you alone, never!

**Thus content and at peace once again,
they love reclaim.**

**The following morning after breakfast, Abradatas,
as requested presents himself before Cyrus.**

Cyrus: Please enter Lord Abradatas.

**Stood before Abradatas was a most regal figure,
strong and resolute he exuded authority and charisma,
with piercing brown eyes, a noble beard and a gentle smile,
he enchanted Abradatas with his aura,
surrounded was he by powerful souls of dignified persona,
all bidding Abradatas a warm welcome with a smile.**

Abradatas: Thank you Lord Cyrus.
(He sat beside Cyrus on a straw mat inclined on a couch)

Cyrus: How was your journey?

Abradatas: Thankfully my lord it was most speedy and happy.

Cyrus: I trust Lady Pantheia's quarters were agreeable?

Abradatas: They were most comfortable.
I am indebted to you my lord.
You are a most gracious and august soul,
for treating Lady Pantheia so kindly
and for returning her once more to me.
My debt to you is eternal,
and I shall forever remain at your disposal.

Cyrus: Thank you Lord Abradatas,
We would gladly welcome any assistance you may offer.
However, please do not feel indebted to us because of Lady Pantheia.
You are free to return with your wife to Susa
provided you promise not to assist Balshazzar and Nabonidus.

Abradatas: My Lord Cyrus, you are most gracious,
and I am forever indebted to your benevolence.
As for Nabonidus and Balshazzar they do not deserve my allegiance.
I would be most happy to serve such a venerable lord as Cyrus.

I am yours to command in whatever capacity you deem propitious.
Although I did notice you have scythed chariots in your army,
being versed in their battle I could join their ranks happily.
And would gladly offer advice on Babylonian chariots most ferocious.

Cyrus: Thank you Lord Abradatas,
I am sure your advice on our chariots will prove invaluable,
with your aid they shall become, a force the Babylonians' equal.
From this day, you are.. amongst us a friend Abradatas.

Part VII
Towards Babylon

The wheels for the decisive battle were now in motion
Babylonia's fortune would soon come to a conclusion!
Cyrus' force numbered some 300,000 strong.
As opposed to the Babylonian men some 350,000 strong.

Cyrus: So Lord Abradatas how do you think Balshazzar
will make his formation?

Abradatas: Well my lord, he is confident of his numbers superior
and as such he shall form a phalanx of 8000 across and 50 deep
and will try to outflank and encircle you I believe.

Chrysantas: Do you think we will be able to break a phalanx so strong
for to counter it stretched shallow we will need to be long?

Cyrus: Well Chrysantas think this:
if the enemy is so far from friend or foe,
to make impact with their numbers more,
then what use is depth of numbers like this?

We shall see the depth of their formation
and accordingly our forces position.
However, if our whole line we bring into play,
we will their superior numbers, out play.

In the van shall be our heavily armed men,
followed by the archers and the spear men.
The initial onslaught will be contained by our heavily armoured men
while the spear men and archers shielded as they will be,
shall rain down their deadly showers upon the enemy.
And in the rear will be stationed our foundation
composed of veterans, each remaining resolute in his position.

What say you my friends of the battle stratagem?

Hystaspas: Well my lord, it appears sound of reason.

Harpagus: I also agree.
And may I suggest using the camels once more against their cavalry.
Their horses when confronted by our camels will run amok and stampede.

Cyrus: Yes Harpagus, the camels I had almost forgotten -
a most potent force, as proved by our Lydian expedition.
Well everyone lets meet early tomorrow morn
so that we can make our final preparation
and head for Babylon.

(Early next morning in Cyrus' tent, all the generals for breakfast gather)
Cyrus: Morning gentleman I trust you all slept well.
So how go the preparations for our departure?

Harpagus: Well Lord Cyrus a little excited for sleep if I must confess.
For at long last we will get to see Babylon and its grandeur.

Cyrus: Well Harpagus I must confess,
I was unable to sleep a wink either.
(They all smile)

Araspas: Well my Lord Cyrus, the troops are ready and most anxious,
to finally achieve a fate most glorious.

Cyrus: Yes gentleman we all have a date
and it does not do well to delay fate.
However first must we make sacrifice to our Lord Ahura Mazda,
for a safe and uneventful journey towards Balshazzar.

**Thus Cyrus makes sacrifice of a bull to Mazda,
beseeching his favour.**

Cyrus: O Heavenly Mazda,
this bull do I sacrifice to you Our Almighty Saviour,
and implore Thee, keep us on our journey safe O Benevolent Father.

**The horn was sounded at midday
and the march was at last underway.
And so Cyrus the Great
led his magnificent warriors towards his glorious fate.**

Cyrus: Tell me Gobyras which is the best route to follow?

Gobyras: Well my lord, there are several which we could follow.
We could take the road that will take us to Babylon's walls near.
That way Balshazzar will see your mighty force and fear.

Cyrus: True Lord Gobyras, but stretched as we will be,
in a long file with the baggage vans without protection
we will be open to attack in such a vulnerable formation.
Balshazzar's forces could swiftly leave the walls of the city
and easily our weak points assail and rush back to safety
before we could aid our vans, stretched long as we will be,

I suggest we march a route away from the walls of the city,
just far enough that they will still be able to view our force, mighty
yet unable to take us by surprise completely.
Should they make a sally,
we would be able to detect it early
and repel it effectively
thus making their retreat costly.

**All agreed this to be a wise move
and so Gobyras directed them to a different route
which on the second midday
brought Babylon in view at a distance safe.**

**Even from afar Cyrus did behold an awe inspiring sight.
Babylon! His heart began to race
as the great emperor never before such a wonder did gaze.
Truly this shall be the crowning glory of his life,
that Providence from birth, Cyrus came to guide.**

Cyrus: What a magnificent sight you are Babylon!

Harpagus: Indeed sire, it pales Sardis into provincialdom!
(Awe struck by its size and proportions)

Cyrus: An undoubted wonder
and that my friend shall be our most glorious prize
but by the looks of Balshazzar's welcome, of such splendour
Babylon is unlikely to yield without a hard fight.

He so speaks as he gazes at the Babylonian troops amassed.
Awaiting his arrival, they were a long while armed and prepared.
Arraigned most resplendent not far from the walls of the city,
they appeared a sight most impressive and mighty.

Harpagus: Indeed sire,
Balshazzar is confident of battle it would appear.

Cyrus: Well Harpagus, let us give Balshazzar
one more day to revel as emperor
it would be impolite to engage in battle any sooner.
We do not wish the great emperor to think us a barbarians horde,
who do not appreciate his welcoming force.
(He smiles)

Harpagus: Indeed sire, that would be rudeness, uttermost.
(Smiles Harpagus)

Cyrus: In any even it would do us good to rest today
and tomorrow test the mettle of the Babylonian pride and joy
and see how they fare against our battle hardened men in open fray.

Next morning Cyrus is out inspecting and conversing with his men
he always made effort, to remember the names of his men,
the importance of which his father in him did instil
from a young age a lesson he never failed to remember still.

'My son you must always treat your men with respect proper
do not view them as expendable fodder.
Remember the course of battle could turn on just one warrior.
Addressing your men by name shows you do not deem them inferior
as such they will hold their king in esteem higher,
feeling proud of the acknowledgement given by their superior
and will in return exert efforts far greater.

Thus seeing a new face he did inquire his name

Cyrus: I do not recollect seeing you before sargent?

Sargent: No sire, for promoted was I to the ranks mature men recently.

Cyrus: And by what name do you go by sargent?

Sargent: Jamshid, your majesty.

Cyrus: Jamshid, a name befitting a handsome young soul.

Jamshid: You are most kind my Lord.

Cyrus: And where do you hail from Jamshid?

Jamshid: From Pasargadae my lord.

Cyrus: Well Sargent Jamshid to live in such a place you are lucky indeed.
Sublime it is with the Empyrean Zagros Mountains for view in all their majesty.

Jamshid: Yes sire, a marvel most heavenly!
Oft, I climb the Zagros, seeking calm and tranquility,
And feel, as if through the eyes of the Immortals I see,
The lush verdant valleys extending beyond eternity,
communing with the Empyreal Horizon lovingly.

Cyrus: Indeed. Providence willing a quick victory we shall gain
and then soon you shall see your beloved Pasargadae again.

**Cyrus converses with a few more of his men
and then retires for counsel with his generals in his tent then.**

Cyrus: Well my friends, the day of destiny is finally arrived!
How is the mood amongst our courageous men?

Gubaru: They are ready to follow you sire, with great pride!
They are excited at the prospect of crushing Balshazzar's men.

Cyrus: And what make you, of the Babylonian force?

Hystaspas: Well my lord, though in appearance a mighty force,
once in battle with our fearless warriors they cross
will quickly take to flight with a heavy loss.
And then we will have to contend with the problem of the siege.

Cyrus: Yes indeed Hystaspas - the problem of the siege.
Well, let us first meet them on the battlefield
and then we shall see how quickly to siege they yield.

Part VIII
The Battle Day
<u>A</u> - Pantheia & Abradatas continued

Unbeknown to Abradatas, his beloved Pantheia
had of gold, his armour[5] made.
Her precious jewels and gold had she bartered as trade.
Also gifted she him, a tunic of princely purple in shade,
and a regal plume for his helmet, hyacinth in colour.

Pantheia: My darling Abradatas before you part to undoubted glory
I have made a gift worthy of your stature and gallantry.

And so she signals to her eunuch servitor
who brings before Abradatas the immortal armour.

Abradatas: My darling Pantheia, you leave me speechless in admiration!
Why and how did you such a gift commission?
For I am unworthy of such a precious benefaction!

Pantheia: Worry not my love, how I acquired the armour.
And there is no man more worthy than you my brave warrior!
(She helps dress him in his heavenly armour)
With you so adorned, I shall bask in your effulgence
which no jewel could ever compare in radiance ....

Abradatas: This day I shall make you proud my Pantheia
and a glorious victory in your name gain,
for no man could claim
to have a wife as devoted as you - Never!

And as he spoke tears gently from her loving gaze fell,
seeing them Abradatas in sweet embrace her held.

Pantheia: My lord, proud was I the day you chose me as your bride.
For that day you breathed life into an empty shell.
You animated my very being with your affectionate caress!
There is no nobler and compassionate soul I know.
Your essence is my drug, without which I would exist no more.
Each time I gaze upon your majesty, I feel blest and full of pride.

---

[5] corselet, armlets, broad bracelets and helmet

Abradatas: My dearest Pantheia fortunate was I
the day I cast my gaze upon you and took you as my bride,
since there is no soul as blissfully happy as I.
And there is no greater joy then having you, me beside.

When I did receive news of your capture
the thought of never holding my sweet Pantheia
ripped my heart asunder.

Plunged was I in the deepest misery.
But by Marduk, you were taken by a soul of the greatest nobility.
Cyrus it is who has filled our lives once more with mirth and glee.
And today he shall receive recompense on the battlefield worthy
of his kindness and generosity.

Today he shall see who it is that calls Pantheia his wife.
O Marduk! Prove me worthy of Pantheia this day,
I beseech Thee disgrace me not this day.
Prove me worthy of such a heavenly soul, that Thou gave me as wife.

Thus the two lovers reluctantly parted.
Abradatas his chariot-box mounted
and slowly drove away
looking back at his beloved one last time, these words he did say.

Abradatas: Fear not my lovely,
for Abradatas soon shall return for his heavenly lady.

She stood there lovingly captivated
until from her view retired her beloved.

(Cyrus early morn rose and made sacrifice to Ahura Mazda)
Cyrus: 'O' Omnipotent Munificent Lord,
Your humble servant beseeches Your support,
Without Your aid victory I could not hope.
Let not this day the tyrants Nabonidus and Balshazzar prevail.
Honour your obedient slave,
and he shall extol your hallowed name above all.
Glory and praise shall be Yours forever more.

And so did Cyrus seek his Lord's succour
and sacrificed a bull to his Lord, to be his chosen victor.
And the Lord answered his plea with lightening and thunder
which pierced the quietude awakening all from slumber.

Cyrus: Thank you My Lord,
glory to Your Illustrious name this day I shall accord
and free your servants from thralldom,
so once again they may praise Your name in freedom.

So, did Cyrus make sacrifice and poured his libation.
And then with his generals did breakfast.
All little nervous for the great battle that they had long thirst,
adrenalin pumping through their veins, they were in a state of great excitation

All were dressed for battle in their resplendence,
garbed in purple tunics,
adorned by bronze corselets and helmets
that dazzled like the sun caught in its effulgence.

Cyrus: Gentleman the day is here.
Today immortalised shall we be forever
as the people who defeated tyranny
and brought to Ahura Mazda glory.

You my most loyal and trusted friends,
I have known most since childhood and some of late.
(Looking at Abradatas Gadatas and Gobyras)
This day victory is within our hands.
A victory Cyrus could never without you contemplate.

I am but a humble guardian of yours.
Your honour and well-being is mine,
as is your pain and suffering mine.
This day shall the glory of Babylon be OURS!

Now my friends to arms and destiny,
for Mazda willing, today we shall revel in victory!
Though they be in numbers great,
they cannot compare to our men so disciplined and brave.

Now go and ready your fearsome warriors,
and let us engage Balshazzar's serf defenders,
who confident in their superior numbers,
will soon flee in face of their vanquishers!

Thus did Cyrus rouse his generals' passions.
Soon the camp was full of commotion for the final preparations.
The cavalry protected their horses,
with bronze frontlets, breastplates and thigh pieces,
as were protected the chariots and men in dazzling armour
Thus the whole army blazed in brilliant splendour
garbed in cloaks and tunics of crimson and purple in colour
and with purple grooved tiara head coverings were the Persians
and in their round felt hats stood firm the Medians.

Soon under the charge of men and beasts the earth would shudder.
O what a fearsome sight of puissant wonder!

Each man with sabre and spear,
Stood ready to battle without fear!

Cyrus' fiery Atash excitedly neighed,
while he all before him surveyed.
Then did he address his army.
To his immediate right was Chrysantas,
commander of the Persian cavalry
and to his immediate left Arsamas,
general of the Persian infantry.

Cyrus: Chrysantas, Arsamas look towards my banner[6]
and follow my stride in like manner.

When they had advanced 20 stadea
they came in panoramic vision of the combat theatre.
Arrayed before them was the impressive Babylonian army.
Mighty in numbers and majestic in appearance
adorned in royal sapphire blue they exuded confidence
outflanking on both wings Cyrus' military

Balshazzar: Look men we have them outnumbered!
Soon, they shall be surrounded,
hemmed in and cut down like curs as they will cower
for daring to challenge my almighty power!

---

[6] a golden eagle with wings spread wide

131

**And so Balshazzar ordered his generals to begin the encircling manoeuvre,
Cyrus having understood Balshazzar's intent advanced to it counter.**

Cyrus: Chrysantas, see how far from their middle
the wings are drawing off, to form the angle to us encircle?

Chrysantas: They are so distant from their and our centre.
They are afraid of their centre reaching us quicker.

Cyrus: Exactly! They wish to encircle us at the same moment.
Once their flanks reach our wings they will try to hem us tight.
But we shall break their confidence with our fight.
Arsamas you slowly with your infantry proceed.
And you Chrysantas follow Arsamas at an even speed
with your cavalry at his tangent.

I will go and look for a point to make our initial thrust
as soon as you hear the horn then press hard both you must
bearing down on the enemy swiftly.
Abradatas with the chariots shall charge through the middle destructively
and you Chrysantas and Arsamas must, to him keep close behind.
Charge through their line
as right behind you will me find.

**So Cyrus moved along the lines bolstering his men's resolve
with words of encouragement he thus spoke.**

Be brave my friends for Balshazzar is no match for your gallantry;
By Ahura Mazda we shall cut through them in glorious victory.
Fight heroically my friends, and show them the meaning of true valour!
Shirk not now, for at your feet shall fall fame, fortune and honour.
Today you shall taste the sweetest victory
for there is no greater prize than Babylon in all history!

Then he came upon Abradatas and greeted him with great affection

Cyrus: My friend having you lead the chariots,
I am assured of victory.
The enemy faced with your warriors shall in fear flee.
The Persians behind shall have full view of your glorious deeds;
and many a song shall be sung of your glorious feats.

Abradatas: You are most generous in praise, my lord.
It is an honour to serve under a king so munificent and bold
I shall do my utmost to prove myself, of you worthy
and hopefully play a small part in your victory
and return your kindness towards Pantheia and me.

Cyrus: Thank you my friend, I am glad to have you an ally alongside,
than to face you as enemy on Balshazzar's side.

Abradatas: So am I for he's not worthy of my men most honourable.
It appears Balshazzar intends to out flank us
and from three sides to attack us.
I wish I was on the flanks than the centre where he's most vulnerable.

Cyrus: Fear not my friend, soon we shall all be engaged in fierce battle and you too shall
play your vital part in testing Balshazzar's mettle.
Charge forth with your valiant soul when you see my signal.

And so Cyrus passed to Hystaspas on the left flank.

Cyrus: Well cousin, strike hard and drive through their right wing,
while I will cut through their left before you can count to three.
(*He says in a teasing smile*)

Hystaspas: Well old man, don't worry about me,
I will be behind their lines before you finish your counting.
(*He teases Cyrus back*)

Cyrus: Well I am always up for a contest.
Let's see how slow this old man is to the test.
(*He laughs teasing Hystaspas back*)
But, just a while rest!

**Cyrus moves along the flank coming upon Xerxes the commander
in charge of the chariots**

Cyrus: Xerxes when you see me charge the fringes of the enemy's wing
then follow suit - Charge with your valour and defeat upon them bring!

Xerxes: You can rely on me sire.
I'll blaze through their flank like hot fire.
(*Cyrus then passes over to Pharnuchus and Artagerses
behind the women's carriages*)

Cyrus: You Artagerses with your camel cavalry
and Pharnuchus with your infantry
in a phalanx attack the enemy on the opposing wing
when you see me charging.
(Cyrus then rides to the left wing, to Harpagus, Gubaru and Tigranes)

Cyrus: Well gentleman, the time is nearly upon us Balshazzar's army
are about to complete their flanking manoeuvres.
When you hear my paean thrust your men forward swiftly,
and on their right flank make them flee like cowardly losers.
Harpagus and Tigranes charge with your cavalry
and Gubaru follow suit with your infantry.

Tigranes/Harpagus/Gubaru/: Count on us sire.

Cyrus: Right gentleman, let's alight their lines with our valiant fire!

**So he rode to the right flank as Balshazzar
had Cyrus' forces completely encircled from afar,
except the rear which was occupied by hoplites, targeteers,
bowmen and charioteers.**

Cyrus: My fearsome noble warriors,
Today the Babylonians shall combat with real soldiers
They like women beguile men by their beauty
however are no match in physical intensity.
(The troops all burst out in great laughter)

They stand between you and glory!
But as soon as they feel your steel,
will crumble under and flee.
So are you ready for IMMORTALITY!
(He cries)

Troops: YES INDEED!!!

Cyrus: Then advance - To Victory! To Glory! To Immortality!

**The whole army join the paean and finally Cyrus cries CHAAARRRGE!!!!!
And lunges his cavalry into battle as the enemy came advancing
thrusting himself at the Babylonian phalanx on the right wing,
he was soon in the thick of hand-to-hand fighting.**

Artagerses in turn followed suit with the camel cavalry
and soon they brought mayhem upon the enemy.
The horses seeing the camels aiming for them did stampede affrightedly.
Carnage was all abound, as the chariots hewed through enemy ranks
on both flanks.
Those that took flight avoiding the chariots were slain by the cavalry
and those fleeing from the cavalry
were in turn slain by the chariot company.

Amongst the mayhem Abradatas and his men rushed with great energy
driving back the opposing charioteers who having no stomach for a fight,
in terror ran in helpless plight.
Brave Abradatas having cut through the Babylonian chariot force easily,
then encountered the dense and mighty Egyptian company,
valiant men who stood their ground
though there were bodies of men and horses mangled all around
as the chariot scythes had cut men's bodies horribly.
In the hellish mêlée some of the chariots overturned,
poor Abradatas was thrown to the ground and was cut and flattened.

And so the Egyptian phalanx advanced towards the Persian warriors.
Their longer spears and shields resting on their shoulders
covered them more effectively than the Persian soldiers
with their corselets, targets and a smaller shield,
and so to the Egyptians little by little they did ground yield.

The Egyptians advanced until they came under fire from the Persian towers,
who thundered down stones, volley after volley
and the archers rained down their deadly showers,
thus was the Egyptian advance checked bloodily.

Meanwhile

Cyrus having broken the Babylonian line
came around and attacked them from behind
Balshazzar, realizing the inevitability of defeat
fled inside Babylon's impregnable walls in retreat.
The Egyptians were left abandoned, alone on the battlefield
surrounded from the rear by Cyrus
who was joined by Hystaspas and Chrysantas.

The Egyptians formed a circle as they closed rank
in order to make their final stand.
Cyrus ordered his men to disengage from hand-to-hand encounter
and to suffer the Egyptians a javelin and arrow shower.
As he mounted one of the towers to survey the battle theatre
he saw everywhere the enemy flee in fear.
And as he gazed at the valiant Egyptian company
in the middle deserted and helpless at his mercy
with just their shields for little protection
Cyrus filled with admiration
at their courageous struggle had pity
and ordered his men to stop their shower most deadly.

Cyrus: Cease men! We have won the day!
It will make our victory no more sweet were we to slay
such heroic spirit and gallantry
whilst their cowardly allies hide inside Babylon in safety.
Gobyras my friend I do believe you speak Egyptian
inform them to surrender
for we have no wish, to such a valiant phalanx slaughter,

Gobyras rode to the Egyptian general and requested they surrender,
but the Egyptian brave and honourable soul, thus did answer:

Egyptian General: How can we save face and be thought brave
for were we to surrender it would upon our name bring disgrace?

Cyrus in response informed them, he and his soldiers
were witness of the heroic efforts of the Egyptian warriors,
for whilst all around them ran in ignominious disgrace,
they fought on in a glorious way.

Cyrus: Join us as allies and not as adversaries,
in return I shall double your pay and grant you lands in our cities.

**On hearing this they decided to join Cyrus' ranks
and so Cyrus gathered all his men to offer them thanks.**

Cyrus: My valiant friends today with the will of Mazda
and your bravery we have defeated the Babylonian Balshazzar
who believed himself invincible but now in fear cowers.
Behind the city walls, of his inevitable end he surely trembles.

I have witnessed many amongst you display fearless valour,
none shied in the facing a force overwhelming in number.
None abandoned their positions,
and all fought like noble lions.
With heroic strength, glorious victory you have gained.
Forever your skill and daring will be acclaimed.
As promised you shall all share in Babylon's spoils before very long,
if Balshazzar thinks he is safe behind his city walls he is sadly wrong.

Besiege Babylon we shall!
Break down its gates we shall!
if it takes till eternity remain here we shall!
Babylon by right belongs to us after our victorious encounter.
Let him stress awhile after his cowardly display, in terror.

**So Cyrus with his generals to his tent retired;
Abradatas was missing discovered.**

Cyrus: Has anyone seen Abradatas,
last I saw he was charging the Egyptian company?

Harpagus: I am afraid not Lord Cyrus.

Gadatas: I am afraid he has joined Mazda's heavenly company
last I saw his chariot had turned over
as he, the dense Egyptian phalanx did encounter.
He and his companions fought most valiantly
until at last they were cut down violently.
I tried to come to his aid
but it was too late.

Cyrus: Poor Abradatas – a most courageous and fearsome warrior
I too saw him charge the Egyptians without fear.
Poor Panthea…
Gentleman to our fallen friend we must go and pay our respects
Hystaspas please find the most precious objects
in our possession that you can find
and follow us behind.

B - Pantheia's Pain

Cyrus with him took animals to sacrifice in Abradatas' honour;
to extol high his name, for his friendship and valour.

When Cyrus came upon the place
where Lady Pantheia had the grave made,
Cyrus saw the lifeless body of his comrade
in the arms of his beloved Pantheia
great sorrow did him overpower
and his eyes welled with tears seeing the two lovers' fate.

Cyrus: I am so sorry, my dear Pantheia.
It pains me to see you and your beloved Abradatas no more.
Though I knew this loyal and honourable soul,
but a short while, there was no doubting his brave and gentle nature.
Woe it is to be parted so soon of such a noble friend.
O Lord why did you bring this most worthy spirit's life to such an early end!

Panthea: Do not worry Lord Cyrus,
for I am to blame for my Abradatas resting here lifeless.
Shame upon my arrogance and honour,
I summoned my Abradatas realising his life would be in mortal danger
O my beloved Abradatas … forgive this unworthy creature ….
Here you lie dead, my most loving and generous husband
for your undeserving wretch of a woman …
(As she speaks she cannot help holding back her sorrowful tears)

Cyrus: My dear Pantheia, do not regard yourself blameworthy,
of Abradatas' love you truly are worthy.
How could a husband be parted of his love most precious?
Life without you would for him have been meaningless.
The only consolation I can offer is that he died in glory,
worthy of his great nobility.

It pains me to see such sorrow inflicted upon your gentle heart, dear Pantheia.
I promise from this day on you have my protection forever,
and like a queen you shall live in honour.

Pantheia: Do not worry yourself my Lord Cyrus,
for it is you that I belong to and had I long ago realised
this day my poor Abradatas would not have died.
It was my misfortune to have been captured by a king so generous.

**As Pantheia finished speaking
Hystaspas with gifts for Abradatas arrived bearing.**

Cyrus: Please my Lady, let me your husband pay tribute
with these small tokens of my friendship and gratitude
and shall have built a mausoleum most worthy
of such heroism praiseworthy.

**Pantheia accepted - and her beautiful beloved
with golden bejewelled bracelets and chains, praise was garlanded
and like the sun he shone with brilliant lustre,
Cyrus also presented his sheathed scabbard gifted him by his father
the day he became a mature man and of men a leader**

**Cyrus and his generals were in awe of Lady Pantheia,
and of her noble and devoted nature,
what a wondrous man Abradatas must have been
to have inspired a love the likes of which they had never before seen.**

**Pantheia bade her eunuchs to leave
only her lady in waiting, Nargis did she behind keep.**

Pantheia: My dear Nargis I have just one last request of you to make.
Promise you shall carry it out without question!

Nargis: Of course my Lady, anything without hesitation.
I am your unswerving servant, you have but to say.

Pantheia: With my beloved Abradatas' departure,
My heart has been torn asunder.
My sorrow is beyond healing.
Without my darling Abradatas, life no-longer has meaning,
with him my desire for life has dissipated.
I can only remain happy alongside him rested.
Promise me, when I lie in motionless state
my and your lord's body you will in the same cloak swathe.

Nargis: My Lady, please do not speak so.
Please do not forsake me in this world all alone,
I shall be bereft without you…. alone.
Please my Lady, do not desert me so…
(So cries she, pleading desperately)

Pantheia: Be brave my dear Nargis! You shall be fine,
Lord Cyrus is a king most kind,
and will take care of you like a sister,
of that have no fear.

So Pantheia unsheathed her husband's dagger
and thrust it deep, in a heart that incurably did ache.
And thus lay united both souls in peaceful repose.
Nargis cried out loud as the two people she loved most,
had abandoned her in a destitute state.
As requested she in the same cloak the two lovers cover.
And then proceeded to drive the dagger and too lay motionless.
The eunuchs in turn honoured their beloved mistress,
by killing themselves as they wished to remain master-less.

When Cyrus got to hear of Pantheia and her servants' sacrifice
he was greatly moved and proceeded to see such love and pride.

Cyrus: What a sombre yet wondrous sight to behold Harpagus,
such love and loyalty - they appear reposed in happiness.

Harpagus: Love is a most wondrous thing Lord Cyrus,
without it we are but empty vessels - rudderless.

Cyrus: Indeed my friend - here a monument to love shall I raise,
to honour their actions in praise.

Part IX
Babylon's Siege & Fall

After great jubilation at the victory
the prospect of a long siege loomed heavily.
For the Babylonians had long made provisions ready
for a siege extremely lengthy.

Two weeks pass by and no progress is made
several efforts are repulsed easily
as no weak points are discovered in the walls of the city
so Cyrus holds counsel with his generals concerning the stalemate.

Cyrus: Well, it has been two weeks yet it remains unassailable.

Harpagus: I am afraid the walls are impregnable
there does not appear to be a weak point anywhere at all,
even if we successfully assault the outer wall,
the inner wall will still stand against us firm and tall.
and then the river Euphrates, my Lord!

Gubaru: True my lord – it appears beyond a frontal assault.
The Babylonians have provisions for three years bounteous… maybe more.

Cyrus: Well then we have a veritable problem,
They are content to wait but we need to move fast gentlemen.
Any suggestions will be listened to keenly,
and considered most intently.

And so Cyrus and the others ponder a while,
and finally on Cyrus' face a huge smile.

Cyrus: There is a strength which is also Babylon's greatest weakness.

Hystaspas: Lord Cyrus?

Cyrus: The River Euphrates, Hystaspas!
We'll dig channels and divert its water,
thus making it fordable and easy to enter.

You Gubaru, shall take one half of the army
and camp near where the Euphrates enters the city

and the other half by Harpagus commanded
will camp where the river flows out of Babylon,
while the non-fighting men by me headed
will be led a little further on
and set about digging a basin to divert its waters
As soon as it is shallow enough attack with your warriors!

Gubaru: That my lord is a plan most masterly!
The Babylonians will never expect such a cunning strategy.

Cyrus: indeed they will not Gubaru!
(He smiles as a man confident of the success of his plan)

And so it was that Cyrus and his engineers
dug a huge basin to divert the Euphrates waters
and made it shallow enough for Gubaru on the night of 12 October
to march his men through the river
and into Babylon without much resistence,
as the Babylonians were taken in a state of bewildering precipitance.

Owing to the huge size of Babylon, most of the city's populace
and army were engaged in festivities most joyous
long after Babylon's defences were breached
the revelers continued partying,
until news of Baylon's taking,
finally all reached.

Cyrus himself later entered
and Balshazzar was completely baffled,
Nabonidus arrived too late
to prevent Cyrus from sealing Babylon's fate,
quickly was he captured by Gubaru at Babylon's gate.
And so it was that Babylonia's star descended,
and its empire faded.

Cyrus entered Babylon to great pomp and cheer,
the people of Babylon received him as their saviour
rather than a foreign victor.
For unlike olden custom Cyrus did not Babylon plunder,
nor did he its people enslave or massacre,
thought it was his right as the vanquisher.
For Cyrus came in peace
and was crowned in the Temple of Marduk as Babylonia's king
by the Babylonian High Priest.
All the priests, princes and nobles bowed and rejoiced at his crowning.

Part X
Cyrus' Human Rights Speech

(Cyrus steps out of the palace and thus addressed the crowd outside amassed)

[7]I am Cyrus, King of the world, great king, mighty king,
king of Babylon, king of the land of Sumer and Akkad, king of the four quarters,
son of Cambyses, great king, king of Anshân,
grandson of Cyrus, great king, king of Anshân,
descendant of Teispes, great king, king of Anshân,
progeny of an unending royal line, whose rule Bel and Nabu cherish,
whose kingship they desire for their hearts, pleasure.
When I well **today** - disposed, entered Babylon,
to set up a seat of domination
in the royal palace amidst, **I thank you all for the** jubilation
and rejoicing.
For Marduk the great god, caused the big-hearted inhabitants
of Babylon to .... me,
I **seek** daily to worship him.

At my deeds Marduk, the great lord, **rejoices** and to me, Cyrus, the king
who worshipped him,
and to Cambyses,
my son, the offspring of (my) loins,
and to all my troops he graciously gave his blessing,
and in good sprit before him we **glorify** exceedingly his high divinity.
I thank all the kings who **sit** in throne rooms,
throughout the four quarters,
from the Upper to the Lower Sea, those who **dwell** in ....,
all the kings of the West Country, who **dwell** in tents, and have brought me
their heavy tribute and kissed my feet in Babylon.
From ... to the cities of Ashur, Susa, Agade and Eshnuna,
the cities of Zamban, Meurnu, Der as far as the region
of the land of Gutium,

---

[7] I have decided not to write Cyrus' words in verse as I wish people to experience the words of the Cyrus himself. I have changed it slightly (in bold) to make it run in the present tense – as he might have spoken to the Babylonians on entering Babylon.

the holy cities beyond the Tigris
whose sanctuaries **have** been in ruins over a long period,
the gods whose abode is in the midst of them,
I **shall return** to their places
and **house** them in lasting abodes.
I **shall gather** together all their inhabitations
and **restore** (to them) their dwellings.
The gods of Sumer and Akkad whom Nabonidus had,
to the anger of the lord of the gods, brought into Babylon.
I, at the bidding of Marduk, the great lord,
shall make to dwell in peace in their habitations, delightful abodes.

May all the gods whom I have placed within their sanctuaries
address a daily prayer in my favour before Bel and Nabu,
that my days may be long,
and may they say to Marduk my lord, "May Cyrus the King,
who reveres thee, and Cambyases his son
remain under their protection ..."

Now that I put the crown of kingdom of Iran, Babylon,
and the nations of the four directions on the head
with the help of (Ahura) Mazda,
I announce that I will respect the traditions, customs and religions
of the nations of my empire and never let any of my governors
and subordinates look down on or insult them until I am alive.
From now on, till (Ahura) Mazda grants me the kingdom favour,
I will impose my monarchy on no nation.
Each is free to accept it,
and if any one of them rejects it ,
I never resolve on war to reign.
Until I am the king of Iran, Babylon, and the nations of the four directions,
I never **will** let anyone oppress any others, and if it occurs,
I will take his or her right back and penalize the oppressor.

And until I am the monarch, I will never let anyone take possession of movable
and landed properties of the others by force or without compensation.
Until I am alive, I prevent unpaid, forced labour.
Today, I announce that everyone is free to choose a religion.
People are free to live in all regions and take up a job provided that they never
violate other's rights.

No one could be penalized for his or her relatives' faults.
I prevent slavery and my governors and subordinates are obliged to prohibit exchanging men and women as slaves within their own ruling domains. Such a tradition should be exterminated the world over.

I implore to (Ahura) Mazda to make me succeed in fulfilling my obligations to the nations of Iran (Persia), Babylon, and the ones of the four directions.

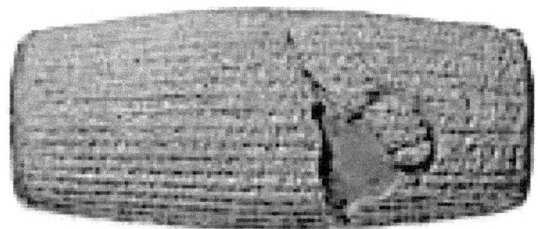

[8]**The Cyrus Cylinder – The First Charter of Human Rights**

---

[8] Can be viewed at The British Museum

Part XI
Cyrus & The Jews - The Anointed One

*(A delegation of prominent Jews headed by their sage Daniel
is received by Cyrus in Balshazzar's palace)*

Daniel: Greetings O glorious and merciful Lord.
I am called Daniel.

(Daniel and his contingent bow)

Cyrus: Greetings my Lord Daniel.
You do us great honour with your appearance at our abode.

Daniel: My Lord is most kind
to so welcome, such a humble soul unrefined.

Cyrus: Nonsense Lord Daniel …for the Divine Light
shines upon your holy soul most bright.

Daniel: My lord I am but a lowly servant of The Almighty
who has come to plead for your charity,
on behalf of my people who have suffered the bonds of slavery.

Cyrus: My Lord Daniel you need say no more
for I am aware of the reasons of your petition.
The Lord has moved me of your people's affliction.
To your Homeland your people are free to return once more
or if they so desire may come with me to my Persia.
Further, for all the kingdoms the Lord has to me entrusted,
to build him a house in Jerusalem in return he has me requested.
As such whosoever wishes to assist in this endeavour,
is free to provide the people of Jerusalem
with silver, gold, and any other possessions,
together with free will contributions
for the Lord's House in Jerusalem.

Daniel: Truly My Lord is The Almighty's Anointed Messenger,
Our promised Liberator.
May The Lord bless you with a life most illustrious,
O Munificent Lord Cyrus.

Thus Cyrus did free the Jews from Babylonian slavery
and allowed them to return to their homeland once more free
And so some 40 000 Jews including the heads of Judah, Benjamin
and the priests and Levites did leave for Jerusalem.
To build once more the Lord's House, with them they brought
many precious gifts, cattle, goods, silver, and gold.
Cyrus gifted them The Lord's Possessions that King Nebuchadnezzar
from his Israelite sacking did plunder.

ACT Five
Part I
533-30 BC - Cyrus' Last Days
(The Campaign Against The Massagetae)

Cyrus having brought the Babylonians under his dominion,
to the eastern frontiers of his kingdom
finally turned his attention.

First in 533 BC Cyrus crosses the Hindu Kush and receives fealty
from the Indian cities of the Indus valley
and establishes Gandhara as his twentieth satrapy.

And finally beyond the River Araxes in 530 BC
Cyrus devised a plan to bring the troublesome tribes of the Massagetae
of the Scythian race under his domination
and thereby eliminating any future threat from this war-like nation.
The Massagetae were by Queen Tomyris ruled
A firm and powerful lady most shrewd.

(Cyrus in counsel with Croesus in his new capital Pasargadae)
Cyrus: My dear friend, I seek your counsel most astute.
By the will of Mazda I have brought many kingdoms under my rule
and now to protect my empire from any future danger
I have to bring the Massagetae under my dominion.
They are a powerful barbarian warrior-nation,
with the potential to challenge our supremacy on the eastern border.

Croesus: My Lord, I have heard their king passed away recently,
and his wife Queen Tomyris has assumed sovereignty.
She might be tempted into union by the prospect of marriage,
with your esteemed personage.

Cyrus: An excellent suggestion Croesus;
but who shall I send to her court with your proposal.

Croesus: How about Lord Harpagus?
He is without doubt a most imposing and persuasive noble.

Cyrus: Harpagus, yes … a friend most loyal and dependable,
and above all most perspicacious and honourable.
Captain Darioush send message to Lord Harpagus,
and say Lord Cyrus desires his company
to discuss a matter which requires his nature most trustworthy

Darioush: As you command Lord Cyrus.

(Harpagus arrives some weeks later in Pasargadae Cyrus' resplendent new capital)
Harpagus: Greetings, my Lord Cyrus, greetings Lord Croesus.
I came as soon as I received your message.

Cyrus: Welcome dear friend. Come join me and Croesus
I hope you had a safe and uneventful passage.

Croesus: Greetings Harpagus,
it has been a long while since I had the pleasure of your company.

Harpagus: The journey was both pleasant and easy.
I am afraid of late I have been rather busy
with appointing translators for our satrapies many.
It has been quite a while indeed since we last conversed Croesus,
I trust you have been kept well entertained by Lord Cyrus.
(He smiles)

Croesus: Lord Cyrus is a most gracious and indulgent, Harpagus.

Cyrus: You are too kind dear Croesus.

Well Harpagus, come join us in our afternoon meal
for you must be tired and hungry after your long journey
I have an important task which I can only entrust you to deal.
It is time we dealt with the Massagetae, our prospective enemy.

Harpagus: A most wise and anticipatory move my lord.
We must bring them under our fold,
for they are far too powerful not to pose future troubles.
I have had reports of frequent raids by them on our eastern frontiers.

Cyrus: Well Harpagus, Croesus has suggested
that their Queen Tomyris may be persuaded
by the prospect of a union of matrimony.
And you my dear friend, I entrust this task, as to her my emissary.

Harpagus: I would be most happy to accept... an ingenious plan Croesus!

Croesus: Thank you Harpagus.
(They continue conversing and enjoying their meal)

Part II
Queen Tomyris

A few weeks later Harpagus finds himself at Queen Tomyris' Court

Harpagus: Greetings O Great Queen of the Massagetae nation.
I am Prince Harpagus of Media, Emperor Cyrus' emissary.
My Lord sends you his warmest salutations, majesty.
Lord Cyrus wishes to make you a proposal,
which shall be to both mutually beneficial.
My Lord Cyrus admires you and your brave Massagetae greatly
and wishes to develop a union of long lasting amity
with you and your people by way of matrimony.

Tomyris: Prince Harpagus thank his Majesty greatly.
However, I am unable to accept such an esteemed offer.
I am but queen of a humble country,
who would feel out of place in a court so much greater and finer.

Harpagus: Your Majesty is most humble, in self-appraise,
for your glorious presence would Lord Cyrus' court illuminate.

Tomyris: Prince Harpagus you are most kind,
nonetheless for my people I must decline.
They are a fiercely proud and independent nation
and would not take lightly to being under foreign dominion.

Harpagus: Your majesty, my Lord Cyrus has no ambition
to enslave or dominate your kingdom;
He only wishes to offer your people his friendship and protection.

Tomyris: That as may be, but we, without protection are quite happy,
though you may thank your lord for his concern and amity.

Harpagus: As you wish your majesty.
(Harpagus and his emissaries bow defeated and leave for home)

151

Part III
To Massagetae Territory

Harpagus back in Cyrus' palace

Harpagus: My Lord Cyrus, I am afraid I bear bad news.
Queen Tomyris your offer of union did refuse.
She is a strong and independent-minded lady,
who is unlikely to your proposal agree.

Cyrus: Such is a pity!
Well we cannot allow the Massagetae to become a stronger nation,
for surely later, they will threaten our kingdom.

Harpagus: Indeed sire, for they already pose great danger.

Cyrus: Well Harpagus we must then check their power!
And so, once more our forces we must ready
and make for Massagetae territory.

After a week's preparations Cyrus' army was ready.
And once more the great emperor marched for glory.
When they reached the River Araxes they began constructing
a bridge for the troops' crossing.
Whilst his engineers were busy building
Tomyris sent a herald to Cyrus
with a message imploring him thus:

O King of Persians be content to rule
the vast empire that you did conquer,
do not be avaricious and cruel
I implore you, do not seek the brave Massagetae to overpower.

O Great Cyrus, leave the Massagetae in peace and liberty,
for should you enter our territory.
It shall bring you nothing but grief!
However as you are unlikely to my advice heed
and are determined to battle seek
then advance three days march from the river
to our side or if you so desire,
an equal distance from the stream on your side retire
and we shall find you, then you shall the Massagetae wrath discover.

Cyrus having read the message, advice sought.
Bar Croesus, all his companions battle favoured.
Croesus remembering the ill-fated battle against Cyrus fought,
the wise words of Sadanis against combat he recalled,
and thus spoke:

My dear friend who rules the mightiest empire ever
with unparalleled justice and generosity
I by Zeus vowed to counsel you with utmost loyalty
the day you showed my household such mercy in victory.
But today as a true friend, I beseech you against military encounter.
For from these uncivilized Massagetae, you have nothing to gain
but a barren expanse of land and should you lose much loss and pain.

From mine own bitter experience I know truly
the heavy price one pays for not being content with one's lot.
My own ambition pushed me too far and cost me most dearly
for my kingdom to you I lost.

Though we all believe ourselves invincible and immortal,
the hand of fate can in the blink of an eye change
and terminate a life-time's accumulation.
I see nothing but danger most fatal.
But should you wish to continue with your campaign
then do it across the river upon their dominion.
For if they become victorious on your territory
emboldened they will press further surely,
whilst should you gain the upper-hand it will be easier
for you to push into their terrain deeper.

Cyrus: My dear Croesus, I have always found
your advice to be most sound.
However on this occasion I must respectfully decline
for I was born not to dwell in comfort my whole lifetime
Providence appointed me to lead my nation
and many others out of serfdom,
To die on the battle-field is my fate
whether it be against the Massagetae today, or Egypt at a later date.
I was bequeathed the task of building the greatest empire ever
and it is my given vocation.... destiny urges me to push further.

You have been a most faithful and trusted counsellor
and today I entrust you to Cambyses, my son elder.
With him you are to return back to Persia.
Should it be the will of Providence that in battle I expire,
than please look upon him as a son and be to him a trusted advisor
as you are to me and he shall treat you …as now …with great honour.
Respect you he shall like the lord you are… of noble birth and character.

Croesus: My Lord Cyrus, you are the most magnanimous emperor;
you have treated me and my family most benevolently
where others would have been predisposed to slaughter.
May the Mighty Zeus grant you victory!
For I shall remain indebted to you and your family forever!

Part IV
Cyrus Thanks His Companions' Loyalty & Friendship

Cyrus: Thank you my dear friend.

Well my friends if this is to be my end,
it is high time I thanked you for the love and loyalty
that you have over the years deemed me worthy.

And should we gain victory
I will owe it all to you and The Almighty,
for He did bequeath me many a friend most virtuous and noble
without whom I could never have achieved such honour and glory.
The Lord has accorded me a life most illustrious and worthy,
one that never could have imagined the king from a nation so humble.

But as you know life is most ephemeral,
before you know it, it leads you to sleep eternal.
I am not so arrogant to think that I possess
any God given right to expect this day success.
If God desires to expunge my life
then so be it, it is His right!

Many kings before believed themselves immortal like the gods to be
and lived their lives in indulgence and extravagance accordingly
while their citizens endured a life of fear, misery and poverty,
suffering punishment for dissension under their lords of tyranny
and I am sure many more who come after me
will also believe themselves gods to be
and intoxicated with unfettered power will rule with cruelty.

But heed my advice if you deem my words worthy,
I have tried to live a temperate life most humbly
though it was within my power to have lived in opulence and luxury.
Had I desired I could have engaged in hedonistic revelry and tyranny!
However, such immoral conduct and forced fealty
is short-lived for there is nothing more worthy
than gaining the respect of one's fellow man through generosity.

As my father oft would tell me:
'Cyrus remember my son the richest man is he
who can count upon the unconditional loyalty
of his friends both in times of peace and danger,
those who pay him homage not out of fear
but out of love, reverence
and deference'.

So, my friends and sons should I fall in battle tomorrow
do not for me sorrow
but rejoice for I have been granted a life most glorious
and been fortunate in having friends most wondrous.

Thus did he his companions thank

Part V
Cyrus Advises His Sons
On The Importance Of Loyalty & Just Rule

(The day before battle in his tent his two sons he thus speak)
Remember my sons with power do you also inherit responsibility
of your family and citizenry.
You are their father and guardian, to serve them is your duty.
Like the father, forgive their transgressions easily.
Be generous of heart in nature
for remember you shall not live forever.
There is no point in hoarding all the gold and silver
for many a precious jewel on this earth will never make a soul richer
for you cannot take them with you at death's bed to the other world over.

Bury not your wealth like the penurious miser
whose heart so impure
prevents him from enjoying his accumulated treasure.
If he only realised the happiness to be gained by having a heart pure!
Munificence towards ones friends, family and many a stranger
is the greatest of joy and pleasure.

I have prized loyalty and righteous behaviour above all
and if I have any innocent harmed,
it was not out of any vindictiveness
but the failings of a fallible mortal.
And those I may have inadvertently wronged,
I would most humbly seek their forgiveness.

Should I fall in battle you Cambyses being the elder
shall inherit my title and with it the world of responsibility.
So my son, do not upon your forefathers name bring shame.
You will have to start afresh and with your actions make your name.
Remember without respect, love and loyalty
of your family friends and peoples of your empire, you will falter.

Treat all as you wish them to treat you in return
assume the path of righteousness for there is none sweeter.
Engender love by kindness of behaviour.
Injustice and tyranny only brings shame and dishonour
and a life lived in perpetual fear and suspicion.

And you Smerdis I shall bequeath the satrapies of Media,
Armenia and Cadousia.
You have been granted sufficient to live a happy and honourable life,
free from the innumerable worries and strife
that accompany being a ruler.
Be loyal to Cambyses for his glory will also be yours as his brother.
Be Cambyses' right-hand, the foundation of his might.
Do not through disloyalty, contrive his demise,
for that will bring destruction and disgrace
upon you too one day!

And you also Cambyses must take care of your brother as the elder
and should never shame or him dishonour
for from him will emanate your greatest strength and power!

**And so entrusting Croesus to his son Cambyses
Cyrus and his army crossed the River Araxes
and into the Massagetae territory.**

Part VI
Cyrus' Dream

As Cyrus sleeps the first night in Massagetae dominion
he dreamt that his cousin Hystaspas eldest son Darius,
who not being of age to go on battle had remained behind in Persia
had grown wings which shadowed Europe and Asia.
He wrongfully interprets his dream as Darius plotting against Cyrus
rather than a mortal vision
foretelling the fall in battle of the Great Cyrus
and the eventual rise of his kin Darius,
and so he summons Hystaspas.

Cyrus: My dear cousin, what say yea,
if I found your eldest Darius, plotting against me?

Hystaspas: My Lord Cyrus, how could that possibly be,
he is barely a youth who has the greatest of affection for his emperor
as if he was his father.
Great shame it would bring upon me and my family,
should a son of mine ever rise against his most noble king,
one who is without doubt the kindest and most generous being;
the chosen one of the gods who freed his people from Median vassalry
and of such a vast empire given them mastery.
My lord if what you say does true ring
then I will execute him myself for his treacherous thinking.

Cyrus: Well Hystaspas, last night as I lay asleep
I dreamt him usurping my throne in Persia,
Darius with two wings I did see
one shadowing my dominions in Europe and the other Asia.
I take this to be a warning from Ahura Mazda
who of dangers in visions often warns me.
Return at once to Persia
and when I return present him before me.

Hystaspas: At once my lord! May the gods grant you a speedy victory!

And so Hystaspas crossing the River Araxes returns to Persia
to keep a watchful guard upon his son Darius,
as Cyrus and his men cross the river
and advance a day's march into the land of Tomyris,
leaving the company of his non-military men behind
Cyrus pressed on, to his enemy find.

Part VII
The Emperor's Fall

However, unbeknown to Cyrus one third of Tomyris' warriors
under her son Spargapises' command fell upon the men left behind,
killing them all gorging upon the feast readied for Cyrus' soldiers
and drank to their hearts content his finest wine.
Gluttonously full intoxicated and merry, fell to peaceful slumber,
for Cyrus' men on their return they presented easy prey.
Spargapises and many of his men did Cyrus' men slay
and even more made prisoner.

Tomyris distraught to hear of the loss of her son in the slaughter
did vow to avenge his death as all her forces she did gather
and came upon Cyrus and his men swifter than soon.
The two forces did engage in furious battle all afternoon
Great slaughter did ensue
with arrows and javelins raining down of piceous hue,
followed by the charging of the cavalries
and fierce hand-to-hand combat reverberating painful agonies.
Eventually did Tomyris' forces victory did claim
as Cyrus' forces regrouped and retreat to fight another day again.
But that was not to be the Great Cyrus' destiny
as after a reign of 29 years in the year 529 BC
he fell engaged in hand-to-hand vainglory
through the heart by a javelin true in its aim was he impaled.
As his life was expiring, his final prayer he made.

Cyrus: My Lord, though I lay here in defeat
I return to you grateful and happy
for you have bestowed upon me great glory
and granted me an honourable and noble end most worthy.
It was my destiny to act as a lesson for posterity
for those yet to come with pretensions to immortality
that no matter how great and might they be
when the appointed hour is near, death they cannot deceive.
And so My Lord I come to You not begrudgingly,
I cannot wait, to You at long last meet.

And as Cyrus finished uttering his last prayer to His Lord,
a Massagetae cavalry officer cleft his head from his body
to present before Tomyris as trophy
and thus was released Cyrus' noble soul
from this temporal world with its petty musings to reflect no more.
His faithful Araspas did in retreat
his Lord's body retrieve
and take his corpse back for burial
in Pasargadae his great capital.

In a small insignificant monument his body was laid in peaceful repose,
one that Cyrus had himself decreed of his humble soul worthy
not a magnificent monument for posterity
to gaze upon in awe.

Cyrus' Epitaph

"O man, whoever you are and wherever you come from, for I know you will come,
I am Cyrus, who founded the empire of the Persians.
Grudge me not therefore, this little earth that covers my body."

Cyrus' tomb

THE END

www.ingramcontent.com/pod-product-compliance
Lightning Source LLC
Chambersburg PA
CBHW080822020726
47501CB00009B/2384